SILENCE OF THE WIND

DAMIEN BUCKLEY

Paperback ISBN: 978-1-917700-10-8

Ebook ISBN: 978-1-917700-11-5

damien-buckley.com

For Laura and Charlotte - thank you for your help and for keeping this secret!

A NOTE FROM THE AUTHOR

Thank you for picking up *Silence of the Wind*! While this novella takes place during the early events of *Orchestra of the Gods*, I recommend you read that first before embarking on this story.

I

Daeven had never heard his daughter's voice, and now he worried he'd lose her forever. He prayed to the Architects that everything would be all right, that they wouldn't take her. He watched the soft pink light of the moon as it crested the tops of the trees, breaking through the clouds for the first time since she'd fallen ill. *It had to be a sign, surely.*

Peneri first felt unwell on the last moon where it hadn't snowed. Neither Daeven, nor his wife, Maera, thought anything of it at first. A simple cold, not even worth troubling the healers over. A good broth of cedar-root and moss, ample sleep, and she'd be well and tending to her chores with everyone else. On the second moon, the fever came.

'I don't like it,' Maera said as she squeezed Peneri's pale hand. Maera had said that every moon since Peneri first fell ill. Daeven had dismissed her at first, the concern of a protective mother. By the fifth moon of her illness, he shared that concern. The three healers in the village had all tried their best to vanquish whatever ailed her, without success. They sent word to a neighbouring village for their healers—some of the strongest in all of Dawan—and he waited impatiently for their arrival.

It would be close to moonset before they arrived, so Daeven did his best to keep busy, to not allow his mind to consider the inevitable. Two of the healers concluded Peneri had shanka—a poisoning of the life force, and one of only a few diseases the healers couldn't cure. The third disagreed, on account of Peneri not displaying any welts on her skin. Maera remained hopeful, holding onto the third healer's words. Daeven... well, he knew. Deep down, he knew.

A child falling foul of shanka would usually be the talk of the whole village. It was so rare, he had only seen it once before in his life. His closest childhood friend, Tan, succumbed to it only a few turns of the moon before they were to travel to Trennale for their Branding. In the end, Daeven made the journey without him. In recent moons, he wished he'd chosen the Orb of Healing. Maybe *he* would be strong enough to heal his daughter. He could have at least tried. Instead, he'd pulled the Orb of the Wind, and that was the moon the world fell silent.

No one was talking about Peneri. Not as much as they might. Something else distracted village life recently. For some, it was exciting. For most, it terrified them.

'Do you think they mean to harm us?' Telmin asked of Daeven, using his hands to convey his words. Telmin could speak and hear, having never undertaken the Branding. Handspeech was a second language everyone learned as a child, ensuring no one became isolated.

Daeven shrugged. He hadn't thought about the bridge and what it might mean since Peneri fell ill.

A hundred moons ago, word came that those who lived in the Old Land were constructing a bridge, and no one knew why. The Great Separation, the chasm that split their lands asunder hundreds of years ago, lay half a moon's walk away. A trio of young men preparing for their Branding stumbled upon the partially built bridge, and soon it was all anyone in the village talked about. What did it mean? Were they in danger? Impossible to answer.

The elders sent scouts to watch its progress, and twenty moons ago those scouts advised of its completion. Many called for its destruction. No good can come of it, they declared. For almost a thousand years their simple way of life had endured. Spoken tales, handed down from generation to generation, told of war and destruction. Times of terror and death that ultimately led to the catastrophe that broke the world in two. The Architects saved them all, so the stories say. So says the story of Dawan, the one chosen by the Architects to offer a life of peace and prosperity, the one the country was named after. The Children of Dawan would come to no harm for as long as they followed his teachings.

Daeven sat at the edge of the stream that ran through the village. It was his favourite thing to do. With nothing on his feet, he would let the water flow between his toes. To most, the water would chill their toes until they were numb. Not for him, or those who had the same ability. He could use the wind to warm the air around him, creating a small pocket of heat that kept out the cold.

He was supposed to be working, but couldn't concentrate. His assigned task was to mill the snow-wheat into flour for food, a chore he'd performed with pride his whole adult life. This moon, he couldn't bear it. He sat at the edge of the water and watched the sails of his windmill turn idly in the breeze. It was his creation, a divine idea from the Architects offered to him in a vision soon after his Branding. He could control the wind. He understood its nature, and he harnessed that knowledge. With the help of the builders—those who chose the Orb of Touch—they pulled the shape of his invention from the stones and trees into an almost living monument that watched over the village. It performed the work of ten men, and he was proud of it.

'I pray to the Architects each moon that Peneri will overcome her illness. Surely even Eraidor himself cannot deny a future to one so beautiful as her,' Telmin said. He mouthed the words as he signed them, as all who still heard the world did. He was a small man with thin features, almost the complete opposite of Daeven, whose broad shoulders carried the weight of the whole world upon them.

'I wish it to be true. I wish it more than my own life. I, too, pray to Eraidor and all the others. I pray they take me in her stead. Her life is worth ten of mine, though I fear Eraidor does not hear me.'

Telmin bowed his head, acknowledging a shared sentiment. 'Have you eaten?'

Daeven pinched his thumb and fingers together. 'No.'

'You must keep your strength. Peneri will need you.'

'I'm not hungry.'

'Then I shall stay here with you until you change your mind.'

Daeven closed his eyes and offered a weak smile and sighed. Telmin was a good friend. What he lacked in stature and hair, he more than made up for with compassion and friendship. He was unbranded. As an only child, he had the right, but he declined. Daeven didn't know why. He'd asked him on more than one occasion, though not recently, and Telmin had never revealed his secret.

As the sky dimmed under the waning moon, an elder by the name of Moel approached. He had a crooked back, a limp, and a smile as bright of the moon itself. He held the whole of Dawanii wisdom in his head. He wasn't *the* eldest, but close enough. 'They are here,' he signed from the other side of the water.

Daeven leapt to his feet and splashed across the stream, not caring to retrieve his boots. He gestured a thank you to Moel as he passed, and didn't wait for him or Telmin to catch up. He ran barefoot through the snow, protected by nothing but a cushion of air beneath his soles, and didn't stop until he reached home.

He threw back the animal skin curtain to his home and into the dome-shaped living area. His whole abode had been pulled and shaped from two giant pines—still rooted and alive—pushing the limits of the bark and wood to create a space large enough for his family. In the distant past, those trees would have been cut and stacked into squares. Destruction in the name of creation.

Inside, two women were in conversation with Maera. Both had orange colouring to their hair, indicating they were from another settlement. Here, yellow was their colour, an homage to the Architect of Reason. Orange was the chosen colour of the Architect of Hope. Right now, hope was all he had, all he could cling on to.

'Daeven,' Maera said, 'this is Reital and Sorell.'

Both women smiled and lowered their heads in respectful greeting. Reital spoke first—with her hands—taking cue from Maera. 'You are of the wind?'

'I am. Thank you, both, for coming so quickly. Please, let me show you to our daughter. I pray you are able to help her.' He didn't wait for a reply. He hurried past them into the adjacent room where they all slept.

Peneri lay on her grass mattress on the floor, covered in many fur blankets to keep her warm. Her eyes were closed and she was restless. Sleeping, but struggling against the illness within her. Sweat poured from her brow, soaking her hair into a matted mess. Her condition had deteriorated in such a short time. Daeven swallowed and looked to his guests, eyebrows raised and knitted together with worry.

Reital and Sorell approached the bed on either side and knelt. Reital was much older than Sorell, though likely too young to be an elder. Both had the same sharp cheekbones and small, slim stature. *Mother and daughter, perhaps?* It didn't matter, so long as they were able to help Peneri.

Sorell spoke using her mouth. Daeven couldn't see her lips well enough to read, so he looked to Maera. 'She asks if we believe it is shanka,' she said as she nodded to Sorell.

'Apologies,' Reital signed, looking at Daeven. 'We need to give your daughter our full attention, which makes it difficult to handspeech. Will your wife be happy to convey our words to you as we try to help your daughter?'

'Yes, please. Anything you can do to help. Please save her.'

Sorell didn't reply. With her hands now free to work, she returned her attention to Peneri. She used her thumbs to open Peneri's eyes, one at a time, and peered into them, their noses almost touching. Reital held Peneri's wrist delicately as if feeling for something. After a while, both the visitors pushed back onto their haunches and looked at each other with grim expression.

'Are our healers correct?' Maera asked, using both her voice and her hands so Daeven could understand. 'Is it shanka? Please tell us it isn't so!'

He didn't need to hear to understand the anguish in her question. He felt it, too.

'There are no lesions, yet all other symptoms are present. This is most peculiar. You were right to summon us, however, I believe we are unable to help. We are sorry to say, your daughter is dying,' Reital said. Her face was without expression. Her words given only as stating a fact, and nothing more.

Maera broke first, tears streaming down her face, her hands clasped to her mouth. Daeven sensed she said something. He didn't need to know her exact words—he knew what she said. All he could do was pull her to his chest and hold her close, sharing in her grief.

'How long does she have?' He used his voice. Though he couldn't hear his own words, he could still speak, although he didn't like to anymore.

The two healers looked at each other before speaking. 'Four moons if she is fortunate. We have done all we can for her. Without our intervention, she would survive no more than the next moon. This may or may not be shanka, but make no mistake, it is no less insidious. We are sorry for your loss.'

'She's not dead yet!' It felt like he shouted. It made Maera jump and pull away from him.

'Yes, of course. Nevertheless, we offer you all our sympathies, and will pray to the Architects she does not suffer.'

'May we offer you some tea before you leave?' Maera asked. Daeven read her lips and forced a smile. It was her way. In spite of everything, in the face of losing their daughter, she still made the effort to be a good host.

Reital and Sorell both stood and declined her offer. 'We must return to our own village. Others will need our help and the journey is long. Again, we are sorry for your loss.'

Maera escorted the two women out of their home, leaving Daeven alone with Peneri. He knelt beside her bed and took her hand in his. It felt so warm, and she looked so small as she slept through her ordeal. He wept for her. *Was there really nothing anyone could do to save her?*

The best healers in the whole of Dawan had tried. Even those without the divine gifts of the Branding offered what help they could. Experimental poultices and potions, fever wraps made from the bark of sacred trees. Nothing worked.

'Why her? She has done nothing to deserve this,' he shouted at the ceiling, calling out to any Architects who would give him audience. 'Please, spare her. Take me instead. I have committed many wrongs in my life, and yet you let me live. Why? Don't punish my daughter when she has made none. Please, I beg of you, save my daughter.'

There came no reply.

He lurched backwards at a touch to his shoulder. He hadn't seen Maera return. For an instant he hoped his pleas were answered. Maybe Eraidor had come to save Peneri. No, it was only Maera. He looked to her with a sad smile, tears blurring his sight as she knelt beside him.

As Peneri lay there, restless, he considered if he would ever see those beautiful eyes of hers again. The brightest, deepest blue eyes. There was a star in the sky exactly the same colour. It didn't belong to any of the named constellations. Indeed, the star didn't have a name at all, not officially at least. He named it Peneri after her. She thought it silly that a tiny speck of light in the sky should have a name, least of all *her* name, but it would always be there, even if she would not. As he thought about that star, a notion came to him. Without a word spoken or signed, he stood and left his wife and daughter behind.

2

Daeven ran from his home through the village, through the stream, still not caring if his feet got wet. As the rush of imagination flowed through his mind—excited by the spark of an idea—he meant to find the elders for permission. Out of breath, and outside their lodge, he stopped. No, they wouldn't agree. It wasn't the done thing, but he had to ask. All other options had been exhausted now. Was he mad? Maybe. He had doubts, though. Outside the lodge he found himself paralysed with indecision. He lost his balance, dizzy—overwhelmed by it all—and allowed himself to fall to the snowy ground.

On his back, he looked for the stars, to find their star, but the clouds had returned. It wasn't a full blanket blocking out the heavens, only thin wisps of white and grey blocking the view as they wandered from west to east in the wind. His star—his daughter's star—hidden. Was that an omen? He hoped not.

A figure stepped into his view, blocking the sky. The last light of the moon lit the man's face. It was Telmin. He offered

Daeven a reassuring smile, then sat in the snow beside him. For a while, he didn't try to speak, only joining him to watch the sky together.

'I mean to take Peneri to Trennale. In the morning at first moonlight,' Daeven said as he caught a brief glimpse of his star before it disappeared again behind another cloud.

'Trennale? Why?'

'It's my only... her only hope.'

'Is that wise? Surely their healers will be no more able to help her than any of the others?'

'I don't mean to seek out their healers.'

They were interrupted by the sound of metal ringing through the trees. The village gong, signalling time for meditation. Though Daeven couldn't hear it exactly, the vibration carried in the wind as well as any sound. He looked at his friend, eyebrow raised. *Had time passed by so fast it was moon's end already?*

Meditation was a ritual every community in Dawan had in one form or another. Here, it was at every moonset before the main meal. The next village over held theirs at first light to mark the breaking of the fast. Trennale, being the largest community in all of Dawan, held theirs only once every twelve moons. This was on account of the sheer number of people who lived there. Families would hold their own meditations on a more frequent routine according to their own preferences.

'Come, let's pray and eat,' Telmin said as he stood, brushing the snow from his furs.

'How can I eat when my only daughter lays in her bed, dying? How can I pray to the Architects when they don't hear me? Don't answer my prayers?'

Telmin only held out his hand, inviting Daeven to take it.

As the gong tolled, the steady bustle of village life swelled into greater numbers as every member of the community filtered from their homes, or their chores, to gather at the centre of the village. It was a large open area surrounded by rounded buildings, their host trees offering a canopy between the ground and the sky. In a way it was like its own building, one with many entrances and rooms. In the centre, a fire was coaxed into life by those responsible for doing so.

Everyone had their place around the fire. Not by design or direction, but by unspoken convention. A collective understanding of the natural order. Reluctantly, Daeven followed Telmin to their place in the congregation. Maera wasn't there, nor would she come. He knew she would be by Peneri's side, and would refuse to leave their daughter to suffer on her own. The sympathetic looks from those nearby told him they shared in his pain.

The village settled quickly and in unison. Every member of the community gathered around the fire turned their attention to the three elders as they took their own places. Yona, the very eldest, raised both hands to speak. He was the tallest in the village, almost absurdly so—Daeven was taller than most, but Yona still towered over him. He liked to wear his furs loose, perhaps to hide his thin frame. Once, he'd been strong and muscular, Daeven recalled from his youth. Now, Yona showed age found everyone in the end, his body betraying him as the years passed by. No one knew his true age, though it was easily one hundred.

'Dear friends, family,' Yona said, arms raised outwards. 'Before we offer our prayers to the Architects, I bring news that I must share with you all. For some time now, our lost cousins across the Separation in the Old Land have been constructing a bridge not ten miles from our village. On this moon, they have completed that bridge, and they have made contact with our neighbours in the next village. This is a momentous occasion for us all. The Architects have seen fit to grant them a way to reunite with us.'

Daeven watched Yona's words with complete attention, unblinking.

'For so long we have been isolated from the rest of the world. Hundreds of years have passed, and while this brings opportunity, we must also be wary. Much can change in a thousand years. We have received word a small group from the Old Land are coming here to meet with us—' Yona stopped mid-sentence, his manner suggesting he'd been interrupted by another.

Daeven noticed some on the far side of the circle were nodding, united in agreement. He caught the words of one of them. 'I don't like it.' More nods of agreement. He looked back at Yona.

'—understand your reticence, however, we must have faith in the Architects. All in this life is of their design. They have willed our cousins to reunite with us, and therefore, I believe there to be good reason. Even still, we will remain cautious. I ask that you all remain in the village and are not to travel to the bridge.' Yona looked knowingly at some of the younger members present, who shrank back with guilty looks.

A ripple of commotion broke through the circle. Daeven turned, along with everyone, to see a young woman running towards them, out of breath, arms waving. 'They're here!' she shouted, over and over. She was alone, so far. Daeven craned his neck to see beyond her for a glimpse of the newcomers. Visitors from the Old Land were the last thing on his mind right now, but even he was a little curious to see these strangers from a long forgotten land.

Yona called for calm, ushering everyone to remain where they were. He stepped away from his platform and approached the girl and spoke with her. Daeven couldn't see her face, and Yona wasn't using handspeech, which left only their body language for interpretation. To Daeven, she appeared excited. She offered no sense of fear or reluctance. Daeven turned to Telmin. 'Can you hear what they are saying?'

'A little. She says there are four men on their way from the bridge.'

'What are they like?'

'How should I know?'

For a brief moment, Daeven forgot his woes and allowed himself to be caught up in the novelty of strangers coming to their community. Had Peneri not been so ill, he would have been up front, there to welcome them. It took less than three heartbeats for that excitement to fade.

How can I be here when Peneri is so ill? I cannot. I just cannot.

Telmin nudged him in the ribs to get his attention. 'Yona is asking for you.'

'I should return to Peneri and Maera. They need me more than some strangers.'

'You will be the elder eventually. We all value your opinion. Maera is tending to Peneri, and there is nothing else you can do for her. So, you need to play your part.' Telmin paused. 'Have you considered they might bring new medicines? New ways to treat Peneri that we have not thought of?

Who knows what new ideas they may have. Exciting times, my friend. You must embrace them.'

Daeven considered his friend's words. He was right, of course. If Telmin wasn't so young, he'd make a good elder. He was far wiser than his age would indicate alone. He placed a hand on Telmin's shoulder and squeezed, then pushed his way through the crowd, past the fire, and joined Yona who now stood stoically alone. Together, they waited for the guests to arrive.

'Do you really think they are friendly?' Daeven asked.

'I am cautious, though, we have not given them any reason to be our enemy. The sentiments of our shared history are centuries old. The Architects have seen fit to reunite us, and I choose to believe it will be for our mutual benefit.'

Daeven didn't share that optimism, although his thoughts were elsewhere, and he had little hope of anything positive right now.

Yona sensed his gloominess. 'The healers told me they were unable to help Peneri. I'm so sorry.'

'I pray to the Architects every minute of every moon—'

Movement ahead on the trail leading away from the village caught both their attention. Four figures appeared. Three wore blue clothing that didn't appear to be made from fur. The fourth, red. *Such strange colours to adorn themselves with.* None had painted their hair, though the red clothed man was blond—a rarity in Dawan—and their skin wasn't as pale as most Dawanii. Daeven considered if they coloured their clothing as tribute to the Architects instead of their hair. *If that were true, then why was one different to the rest?*

'They are armed,' Daeven noted, nodding at the spears the ones in blue carried. The spears were all a head taller than the men who carried them, and they looked rather impractical. Too long and too heavy for hunting.

Yona allowed the four to approach, not moving from where he stood. Daeven saw the whispering of those around him. He could tell they were mostly nervous, yet at the same time eager to see what these visitors brought. What their presence would mean for their future.

The man in red spoke, holding out his hand, thumb on top. Daeven didn't understand the gesture, nor what the man said—his lips weren't easily read—and the man didn't use handspeech. After a brief pause, the man lowered his arm, as if disappointed to not received an expected response to the gesture.

Yona spoke so Daeven could understand. 'We welcome you, Humbold, and your companions to our humble village. I must say, we were all most interested and surprised when work began on a bridge after all this time. We have prayed to the Architects that this is the beginning of a new friendship between us.'

'I am told,' Humbold said, Yona signing the words for Daeven, 'the Architects came to our great queen in a dream. They demanded she build the bridge in their name. We therefore come in peace, and are comforted you share in our love for the Architects and their teachings. I have been tasked with meeting you this moon. A brief visit to demonstrate we mean no harm, and to extend an invitation to your queen to come to Miar Lenns. Forgive me, you *do* have a queen?'

Daeven questioned that last word to Yona, who shrugged ever so slightly in reply.

'Forgive us,' Yona said, 'we don't know that word. This is only a humble village. If you mean to meet with one who speaks for all of Dawan, we have no such person. Our largest settlement is a walk of two moons from here. Their elders are considered the wisest in Dawan. Perhaps it is those your... queen will wish to speak to.'

'Two moons by foot is more than we are prepared for. We will return to our city and arrange another meeting between us.'

Yona nodded his agreement, then offered the four to stay for the evening meal, which they gracefully accepted. He invited the gathered villagers to celebrate the beginning of their new friendship. Daeven, while heartened to see the strangers weren't hostile, was in no mood to celebrate. It didn't feel right when Peneri was so ill. He excused himself.

The talk of a two moon walk to Trennale sparked a fire within him. He couldn't wait until moonrise. As he considered the logistics, he brightened, his mood lifting. It was a ray of hope in an otherwise bleak future. He rushed through the animal skin curtain, found a carry skin and filled it with dried meat. He moved around the room with haste, ignoring Maera until she forcefully took him by the arm, making him stop.

'What are you doing?' She wore a confused expression.

'Trennale,' he shouted. 'I will take Peneri to Trennale. I will ask their elders for her to be Branded. It's the only way.'

'Daeven, you can't! She's too frail to move.'

'I will carry her. Every step of the way if I have to. If I do nothing, she will die, and I won't be able to live with myself.'

'Trennale is two moons away. If the Architects will it, she will come through this.'

'If the Architects will it? They teach us to lead our own lives, make our own decisions. I have decided. I *will* take her, and I will take her right now.'

'Yona hasn't agreed to this, surely?'

'I haven't asked him. I don't need his permission to save our daughter's life.' He knew he was shouting, despite not hearing his own words. He gathered whatever he could, whatever he thought he might need on the way. It would be a difficult journey, but it was one he knew he had to make.

3

Maera was right. Yona would never sanction him taking Peneri from the village and all the way to Trennale. Thankfully, Yona—as well as almost everyone else in the village—would be distracted by the visitors from the Old Land. He wouldn't have long, but he could be well on his way before anyone would notice he was gone.

'You're not even going to tell them?'

'No. As you said, Yona would never sanction this. Trennale is her only hope. You know I have to try.'

She inhaled deeply, readying herself. 'If I can't stop you, then I'm coming with you.'

Daeven took her by the shoulders and pulled her into an embrace, hugging her tightly. She always smelled so good, her hair washed with moon-petal oils. A tear fell onto her shoulder before he gently pushed her away. 'No, you have to stay here, allow us the time to get far enough away that I cannot be turned back.' He could feel the words catching in his throat as he realised this would be the first time in his life they would be apart from each other. *Two moons there, two moons back.* He could manage that. For the good of his family, and the life of his beloved daughter, four moons was a small price to pay.

In the end, he gave Maera no choice. He would go without her blessing also, though he knew she would not stop him. He would have to carry Peneri on his back, and drag his supplies by rope behind him. The only other option would be to steal one of the wheeled carts used for moving food from the farming lands into the village stores. That wouldn't do. No, carrying her was the only way.

Not since Peneri was an infant had he carried her. Though even now at twelve, in her frail state, he was surprised by how light she was as he lifted her from her sick bed. Reluctantly, Maera helped her onto his back and wrapped them both in a cloth sling—as they would a baby—to help support her weight on his shoulders. Daeven's huge frame easily supported his daughter, though the sling would keep her tight to him.

Peneri slept through the whole ordeal, and the only way he knew she was still alive was her warm breath on the back of his neck as she nestled her chin on his shoulder.

'Can you remember the way?'

He nodded. Even though it had been almost twenty years since he last visited Trennale—for his own Branding—he knew the path as if it were part of his soul. It was like there was something ethereal that connected every living soul to that place, and no one understood how or why. Even those who had never been there before would somehow know the way and not get lost.

As he prepared to leave home, it all suddenly felt very clandestine. Maera peered around the curtain that separated them from the rest of the village. Satisfied there was no one in the vicinity who would see them, she waved him out.

'Please be careful, and bring her home safe and well.'

Daeven kissed Maera on the cheek and left her behind. He couldn't bring himself to look back at her as he knew he'd cry. Peneri was his only concern now, and this would be his greatest trial.

There wasn't anyone around, yet he still felt guilty as he made every effort to keep himself concealed from anyone who might stumble across them—no easy task with Peneri strapped to his back, and dragging a heavy sack through the snow. The trail it made would make him easy enough to follow if they so chose. He doubted anyone would, though. Once clear of the village, they would be on their own, for better or worse.

No sooner than they were alone did he truly realise the scale of the task he'd set for himself. He'd not left the village for many years. Only twice had he visited Trennale, and neither of those occasions had be been alone, nor without his hearing.

Away from the fire torches of the village, the forest felt tighter and more lonely than ever. The canopies of the trees blocked out any remaining vestiges of moonlight, and there were no stars to guide him. All that lit his way were the insects that lived in the vegetation. Their gentle purple light rippled outward with every step he took. A patch of gentle illumination no more than ten paces in any direction.

He missed hearing the sound of animals and birds. They were always there—in abundance—and he knew they were still there now, yet they may as well not be. Frightened, he trudged on, the weight of his daughter pulling on his back. She weighed little, but miles of uneven terrain wore on him.

Peneri remained asleep the whole way so far. He knew he'd need to wake her soon—she would need water, and the medicine the healers had left for her. Nowhere felt safe to stop, though. Direwolves and other dangerous animals lived within these trees. He was surprised he'd not seen any so far, reasoning they must prefer it farther east where it was a little warmer and with less snow. He was heading north and west, where it was both colder and darker.

Exhaustion eventually got the better of him, forcing him to stop and rest. One tree would be as good as any other, for they all looked the same— tall, thin pines, all reaching for the stars. He chose one that grew out of a shallow incline. It offered a little respite from the wind that forever persisted everywhere in Rybban. He laid down the only fur blanket he'd brought with him, and lowered Peneri onto it after kicking away as much snow as possible.

'Papa?' she mouthed, her eyes half open, confused. Oh how he longed to hear her voice, even once.

'Hush now, my sweet child. Papa's right here.' He smoothed the damp and matted hair away from her brow. Her skin was so hot to his touch, and it worried him. It was so dark now the insects had stopped illuminating his steps, he could barely see more than a silhouette of her against the white of the snow. *Was I right to bring her? Have I made matters worse?*

There was no going back now. He understood the toll this journey placed on both of them. No, the only way was forward. He made Peneri as warm and as comfortable as possible. He closed his eyes and focused the air around him, creating a wall of near invisible protection to keep the wind from reaching them. Using his ability for long periods would exhaust him far more than trekking with a child on his back, but his well-being wasn't as important as Peneri's.

Through the canopy of the trees above, he saw a small section of sky, and within that gap sat a single, solitary star. It had a red tint to it, and it twinkled. He couldn't tell if the star belonged to one of the constellations or not, though he drew comfort in the belief they were not truly alone. The stars represented everything the Architects ever were or ever could be, and if he could see even one star, he knew they would be watching over them.

He stared at the star and let his mind drift back to better moons gone by. There were three perfect memories of his life. The moon of his Branding, the moon of his joining to Maera, and the most perfect of all—the birth of his only child.

Neither of Daeven's parents were Branded, as they were not the eldest in their line. He was their only child, so that right was his to claim. At first, he declined the invitation to Trennale. Of course, eligibility for the Branding was a privilege open to so few, and those who survived it were held in higher esteem in their communities. Half who underwent the ceremony would not live to see the next moon. That wasn't what worried him the most.

'What if I choose the Orb of Immortality?' he'd asked his mother. She was the strongest woman he'd ever known. Not in the way the builders who chose the Orb of Touch were, but strong-willed and a force of nature even his father had been afraid of.

'Is that so bad? Many desire that orb, to live for all time. Imagine how much of the world you could see if you had all of time to see it?'

'I'm happy here in the village. I don't need to see the

world to understand my place within it. I couldn't bear to outlive you all. To see my children die, and their children born, grow old and die also. I think that would become a very lonely life.'

His mother smiled and stroked his cheek with the back of her fingers. 'You are wise beyond your years, Daeven. Though, you fret over impossible things. No one has ever pulled that orb from the flame.'

'Except one. I know you've heard the stories, too.'

'Yes, but it's only a story. No one has ever seen this person. No one has ever known a man or woman to live much past one hundred.'

'Maybe they went to see the world.'

'Maybe they did.'

In the end, persuaded by his mother in particular, he undertook the Branding and selected the Orb of the Wind, and that was the last moon he heard his mother's voice. It was also the same moon he met Maera. She witnessed his ceremony, though, she too wasn't Branded. She'd been there to witness her brother's Branding. Daeven remembered a thin young man who looked just like her, if he half-closed his eyes. Aelene claimed him that moon after he chose her orb. Daeven consoled Maera in the morning light of her brother's death, and they discovered a connection that would keep them together. Until this very moon—the first they'd ever spent apart.

He had to leave, though. For the life of his daughter he would try anything. If she could find the strength to pull an orb for herself, she had half the chance to survive. Those who were Branded and survived were cured of all their ails as their bodies were imbued with the power of the Architects themselves. He hope for her the Orb of Healing, so that she may live and help others to heal. Peneri loved to help others in any way she could. It was only right, now, the Architects chose to help her.

'Please don't let her die,' he said, half dreaming, half watching that tiny red dot. 'She's innocent in everything in this life. She's too young. Please, take me in her place.'

Of course, there was no reply. The two of them were alone, a long way from anyone.

The moon of Peneri's birth came early. All of the healers in the village had agreed she wasn't due for five more moons. No father should ever miss the birth of his child, but he almost did. That moon—and for the first time in his life—he'd taken a walk to the edge of the Separation alone. He didn't know *why* he went. It was as though something in the wind called to him, spoke to him in a way nothing else could. He'd never been back to the Separation since, either.

This was long before the bridge, and long before anyone had the notion of meeting the lost people on the other side in the Old Land. The Separation was a huge canyon with rough, plain and jagged edges made of a pale brown stone. The sky was lighter here and it hurt his eyes. A hundred generations of living in darkness had forced their eyes to grow accustomed to the perpetual night. Here at the edge of the canyon, it almost felt warm. Almost.

Below, many hundreds of feet beneath him, water flowed. For so high above, it looked like nothing more than a trickle. The elders spoke of vast plains of water that bounded their lands. The rivers and streams all led to these oceans. Some had even tried to conquer these waters and float like leaves on a pond to discover distant lands. None who tried survived, the waters too vicious and dangerous to make it far enough.

On that moon, as he looked across the crack in the world, as he imagined what life was like over there, he swore he heard a voice call to him. The first voice he'd heard in any time since his Branding two years earlier. Whispers of a woman carried on the wind, telling him to go home. Telling him he was needed. If it wasn't for that whispering, he would have stayed until the moon disappeared below the horizon way across in the Old Land. If it wasn't for that voice, he would have missed his daughter's birth.

As it was, he made it home mere moments before she arrived, all red and blotchy as she emerged from her mother's womb, helped by a female healer. That was the first and only time he regretted his Branding, as he knew he would never hear his daughter's voice.

All these memories swirled around his mind as he forced himself to stay awake. He couldn't afford to sleep. *Only I can keep watch over you.* He must have slept, though, as the first light of a new moon broke through the trees ahead.

He snapped himself fully awake as he realised Peneri was no longer asleep and delirious. She sat upright, her back against the tree, watching the moonlight filter through the trees. It made for an eerie sight, as if the light itself was pouring into her.

She turned to look at him, and he scooted over to her. Even in the pale moonlight her pallor was awful, with dark shadows under her eyes as though her very soul was draining from them. It made her look old—an elder without the wrinkles and grey hair. As she moved her head, only then did he notice the pustules forming near her ear. *It is shanka, after all.* His lower lip quivered as he tried to force a reassuring smile.

'Papa,' she signed, her hand movements slow and unsteady. 'Where are we?'

'I'm taking you to Trennale.'

'Why are we going there?' She turned her head, wincing. 'Where's Mama?'

'I'm taking you there to make you better, if the Architects will it. Mama stayed at home. It's only you and me here. Don't fret, I will keep you safe and make you well again.' He did everything he could not to cry in front of her. The hurt behind his eyes had to stay hidden, and he hoped she didn't understand how gravely ill she truly was.

'Why Trennale? What's so wrong with me our healers couldn't help?'

He really didn't want to answer, but she repeated the question with her hands over and over. 'Why?' Eventually, he relented.

'I wish for you to be Branded. It's the only way now. I mean to ask their elders to place you in the hands of the Architects, and plead for your health and recovery.'

Peneri jerked to a sitting position, the agony of her stiffness on full display. 'Branded? No! I refuse. I don't want to be Branded. I never wanted to. And I'm too young, anyway.'

Daeven laid his hand on her arm to stop her speaking. 'It's your only hope. We cannot lose you. I *won't* lose you. You have shanka, and if I don't do this for you, you'll die.' He couldn't hold back the tears any longer.

It was Peneri's turn to take her father's hand in hers. 'I feel fine, better, in fact. I want to go home. Please.'

For a moment, Daeven considered if she really was recovering, and not almost ready for Aelene to claim her. The pustules on her skin told him otherwise. 'Look at your hands,' he said. He took her hand in his and indicated to an angry, red boil on her knuckle.

'It's nothing,' she said, pulling her hand away to gesture the words. 'An insect bite, or a nettle sting.'

Daeven shook his head and made a circular motion around his face, then pointed to hers. She didn't want to believe it, and he desperately wanted to share in that disbelief, but he knew the truth. Her bottom lip quivered as she felt around her cheeks with her fingers. He knew she could no longer deny it.

'I still want to go home. I don't wish to be Branded. If I am to die, then I want to be at home with you and Mama.'

'You *are* with me. I love you, and I know what's best for you. You may be ready to give up so easily, but you are still so young. It's my role as your father to keep you safe from harm. To do what's necessary to protect you. You'll listen to me, and we *will* go to Trennale.'

'I could still die anyway, if that's what the Architects wish.'

'If the Architects wish it, then so be it. But it's right that we ask them. I refuse to believe this cruel disease is the will of any of the Architects, not even Sarratenian. We will go to Trennale, and we will ask them. We are good people. You are a good person, a girl who's barely lived. I know they'll help us.' He rose to his feet and offered his hand.

Peneri didn't move at first as she contemplated his words. Eventually she conceded and made to stand, but collapsed under her own weakness.

'I will carry you. I have brought you this far, and I will carry you to the end of all Rybban to keep you safe.'

4

The moon had cleared the horizon by some way when the great mountain came into view in the distance. Trees had protected them most of the way, but now they walked through a wide open snowy plain. The wind bit harder, although it made it easier to keep watch for direwolves and other predators. There were more trees ahead, and the mountain rose in the sky beyond them like a shrine to the stars themselves. He guessed they would reach Trennale by the time the moon reached its zenith.

Peneri had gone quiet in the last mile or two. Not through words, as he couldn't hear or see them with her on his back. No, her movements had fallen still. No small shifting of an arm or foot. Asleep, perhaps. Her hot breath still tickled the hairs on his neck, so he knew the worst hadn't come.

Trennale seemed smaller to him now than the last time he'd been there. Back then, he was on the cusp of manhood, and it had been the first time he'd left his tiny village. The mountain, with its twin peaks caressing the clouds, loomed over everything and everyone who lived below. This was what the Old Land called a city—a word that had stuck through the centuries. Trennale was the centre of everything, not a place of pilgrimage. No, that distinction belonged to the Sisterhood—another walk of two moons farther north. Once, he'd longed to visit them himself, though that urge had faded with age. His life was his family and his community. Until Peneri fell ill he thought he had everything he could ever want. Now, he'd left that life to protect it, and brought his daughter with him to protect *her*.

As he cleared through the trees and picked up the well-worn track that led into the depths of the city, he recognised the rope and wood gantries that hung in the trees above. They didn't look safe or appealing to him, much preferring to keep his feet on solid ground.

To his left as he walked, exchanging welcoming looks with some of the people who lived there, he noticed two homes created from the huge pines they belonged to had been destroyed. Efforts to repair the damage were underway —a dozen builders carefully clearing away the damage and teasing the earth and wood into a new wall. Building wasn't a fast process, he knew. The stone and wood required gentle encouragement to become a new shape, almost as if permission was needed from nature itself. Pull or twist too fast, and the wood would tear, or the rock beneath you shatter in explosive reaction, as if fighting back. It was fortunate, then, that builders felt no pain should they find injury in their work.

A middling-aged woman with the same red in her hair as all from Trennale scurried over to Daeven when she caught sight of him. His own yellow painted hair telling all who saw him he was a stranger to their home.

'Welcome to Trennale,' she said with a smile. She had uneven, grey teeth, and held her head at a slight angle to her left.

Daeven replied with a thank you, using his hand. The woman immediately understood, and continued in handspeech.

'Welcome,' she said again. Her smile lowered into a look of concern as she noticed Peneri on his back for the first time. Daeven was taller and broader than the woman, and his and Peneri's furs matched in colour, so she was well hidden on his shoulders. 'She is unwell?'

'I fear she is dying. We have travelled two moons here to seek help. Would you please escort us to your elders?'

'Elders? She needs a healer. I am Unbranded, but I know where to find the best of us. Come, follow me.' She turned to walk.

Daeven tapped her shoulder to regain her attention. 'She is beyond healing. We have already tried. I *must* speak with your elders. Only they can help her now.'

The woman seemed reluctant, but eventually conceded and led him onwards.

As they walked, Daeven noticed more damage on both sides of the path. The gantry ahead had broken, and a handful of men and women were busy effecting a repair. He tapped the woman's shoulder again. 'What happened here?'

'Dragons,' she said, stiffening slightly. 'Their attacks grow more frequent and more vicious.'

He had, of course, heard of dragons, though he'd never seen one. The elders regaled their villagers with tales filled with the tiny creatures. Usually, they were shy and elusive, and if you were ever to see one, it was a sign of good fortune coming your way. Dragons were beautiful, blue animals that graced the skies with an elegance that birds couldn't offer, capturing their prey with spittle that turned to ice on contact.

He found it hard to picture what they looked like in his mind. Some said they were little more than snakes with wings and claws, while others said they were eagles with skins of leather. They wore no feathers, and their tails snapped like a whip. These stories captured his imagination as a boy, and he'd longed to see one his whole life. He'd never had more than a meagre amount of good fortune, and he wondered if the dragons had anything to do with that.

Maybe if I see one here, it will bless us both. As he considered this, following the woman, the scale and severity of the damage around him challenged the stories he'd been told.

As he walked deeper into the centre of the city, he was reminded how vast Trennale was compared to his village. His home numbered more than one hundred and fifty—give or take. Here, well, ten of his village would fit within the foot of the mountain with room to spare. Residents were numerous, mostly with red in their hair, though there were many with other colours indicating they came from other settlements across Dawan, just as he did.

Soon, a familiar structure loomed ahead. To him, it resembled a smaller version of the mountain to his right—not in shape, but as a presence that stood imposing over everything else around it. This building, carefully crafted from a mix of moulded stone and wood blended together like a half-stirred pot of oatmeal, stood far apart from all others.

The last time he was here was on his Branding moon all those years ago. He thought most of his memories of that moon had been lost to time, but as he stood at the entrance, that whole event came back to him with perfect clarity. The moon had shone brighter back then, too. He was sure of it. Maybe it was only the innocence of youth and hope. He'd not been scared, even with the thought of choosing either the Orbs of Death or Immortality swimming through his mind.

When he first learned of the Branding, long before he had to make his choice, the thought of it maybe killing him terrified him. 'Why would anyone choose to die?' he'd asked his father as he listened to him speak of the ritual.

'One should not be afraid of death. This short life bestowed upon us is but a mere step compared to the journey that lies before us. Aelene takes us all in the end, even the elders, eventually. Those who pluck her orb from the flame are the most special. They are called to the next life to be with their forebears, for the Architects have great plans for them.'

'What plans? What do we do in the next life? What's it like there?'

'Ah, now *there* is a secret, one that none of us really know. Not even Dawan himself knew the whole truth.'

'Dawan knew everything, I thought. He had the ear and the heart of the Architects themselves. All the stories say so. Dawan was the closest anyone came to being an Architect in their own right.'

His father laughed at that. 'Perhaps that was so, but still he did not know everything. He was the best of us, and if it were not for his wisdom and might, there would be no land named after him. You, nor I, would not stand here and draw breath this moon. No, there would be nothing. The Architects blessed Dawan in a way no others were. We are all his children, and we owe him all our lives.

'When it is your turn to be Branded, whichever orb you

pick has already been chosen for you, even now. You honour the Architects by finding the courage to accept their gift, and surrender your tribute in return.'

'What if I choose *not* to be Branded?'

'That is also your right. Perhaps the Architects already know if you will or will not.'

'Then what is free will? If they already know everything about us, what decisions we will make or not, then what is the meaning of life?'

'And therein lies the lesson, my son. Life is full of difficult questions, and we as mere mortals are not meant to have that knowledge. We must have faith that the Architects know what is best for us. Be Branded or not, however you decide is by their will and with their grace.'

In the end, Daeven went on to choose the Orb of the Wind, and he did so willingly. Now deaf, he still hears his father's words as clear as the moment they left his lips. He missed his father, and only now as one himself did he understand his role in life.

He observed the entrance to the sanctum and drew heavily through his nose. Before he took another step, an old man exited through those doors, accompanied by a far younger woman. Daeven remembered that man, though not his companion. Orratan—one of the elders of Trennale—stood before him with welcoming arms. He was as grey as any man could be, save for the lick of red paint in his thinning hair. Daeven remembered him being taller on his last visit.

The young woman spoke, using both her mouth and her hands. "Welcome, son. What ails the child you burden on your shoulders?"

Daeven knew they were not her words, but Orratan's, so

he turned to the old man for his reply. 'We fear she has shanka. I have travelled far with my daughter on my back in the hope she can be rid of this terrible affliction.'

Orratan stepped forward. "Such a long way to travel. Your own healers were unable to help her, I presume?"

'They could not. Even those from our neighbouring village were unable to do little more than prolong her health so that I might bring her here.'

"Our healers are no more able to cure shanka than any other."

'I knew that to be true.'

"Then why burden yourself with the journey? Why put your daughter through this trial too?"

'I came to seek her Branding.'

Orratan helped Peneri from Daeven's back and onto the ground. The old man appraised her condition with vigorous attention to detail. 'You are correct, it is shanka. There's no doubt about that.'

The words startled Daeven as he realised he *heard* the words. It had been Orratan who spoke, he was sure of it. The words had been pushed inside his head like a thought. And then he remembered—Orratan had the power of telepathy, surrendering his actual voice. Out of all the gifts the Architects bestowed upon those who were Branded, those linked with the mouth and ear were the only ones that necessitated the use of handspeech.

So few members of any community or clan would select the Orb of the Mind, or Orb of the Wind. After the Orb of Death, the Orb of Touch was the most commonly chosen, by almost half. The Orb of Healing appeared in one in twenty Brandings on average. The rarest—aside from the Orb of Immortality—was the Orb of Foresight, and there may only be one of those for every three villages. Seven orbs in all, and all but Aelene's would save Peneri from succumbing to this terrible illness.

'How old is she?' asked Orratan as he stood, his examination complete.

'Twelve, by the old measure,' he replied, thinking his answer. Most villages still measured the year by the position of three stars at moonset, relative to the horizon.

Orratan shook his head. 'I cannot permit it. No one so young has ever participated in the Branding. The body must be fully grown to withstand the power contained within the orbs.'

'She will die otherwise. This is my... her only hope. *Please.* There must be a way.'

'The teachings of the Architects are precise. Even I cannot overturn them. I'm sorry. I will pray for your daughter and your family. All I can offer you is lodgings to make you both comfortable here in Trennale. I fear she would be too weak to withstand a journey home.'

'I can't! I refuse to believe there isn't another way. She must be Branded. She *must!*'

Daeven scooped his daughter from the ground into his arms in one swift, practiced motion, then pushed his way past Orratan and his companion. He turned his back to the sanctum and used his shoulders to push away the heavy curtain covering the entrance.

Inside was a long corridor he knew led to the great auditorium at the rear of the building. There were many rooms leading off the corridor, but he was only concerned with making it through to the outside. He ran, as fast as he could go, burdened with the weight of Peneri in his arms—more awkward to move than it had been with her on his back.

Behind him, Orratan and his companion would be following, though he didn't turn back to check. He couldn't hear if they were calling after him.

At the end of the corridor was another animal skin curtain—two, in fact, pulled together at the centre. He shielded Peneri's face as he charged through, brushing the leather aside as though it was nothing. Dozens of eyes fell upon him as he pulled himself to a stop.

Many imposing grey statues gazed down on him, each representing one of the Architects. Each the height of three men, their cold stone eyes surveyed the open auditorium, they themselves watched over by the stars and moon. Architects watching over Architects, watching over the humanity they created.

Each statue stood sentry in an elongated circle. Amser—the Architect of Time, Eraidor and Aelene—of life and death respectively. He knew most of them, though there were still some that Daeven couldn't name on sight. Those were not all who watched him now.

In the centre were more faces, human faces, all turned to see who had interrupted them. They were gathered around the towering, twisted monument that had the power to Brand someone and alter the trajectory of their life, or indeed, end it. A family, a mix of both young and old, all with red hair, watched Daeven as he staggered a few steps farther before falling to his knees, exhausted. He'd made it. He'd brought Peneri here, and now realised that he was unable to save her.

5

Daeven sat on the cold ground with Peneri cradled in his lap. She was asleep, her breath misting gently. He stroked her hair away from her eyes, and wept as he realised the folly of his actions. Maera was right—she should have stayed at home and kept warm and comfortable in her final moons.

Those around the monument came to them, offering assistance, closely followed by Orratan and his companion behind.

'I thought I could save her by bringing her here,' he said. He spoke with words, hoping they were understood.

Orratan ushered the bystanders away before sitting beside Daeven. 'Our offer remains,' he said, pushing the words into Daeven's mind. 'We can make her comfortable here for as long as she needs. Our healers will not be able to cure her, but they can take away her pain.'

'Can they take away my pain, too? No father should see their child suffer in this way. Why did the Architects see fit to create an illness so cruel? Why do they bestow the gift of healing, yet allow this disease to thrive?'

'As old and wise as I might be, I don't have all the answers. We can only trust in them that they know what is best for us all. Come, you must be hungry after coming all this way.'

He wasn't hungry, and he was reluctant to move. He conceded, though, and allowed Orratan to pick Peneri up and carry her—a brief respite from his own burden, though he didn't let her out of his sight.

Orratan took her to a small room within the sanctum where she was laid on a bed made of layers of furs. The room itself felt uninviting and lifeless, with only a small window and nothing else in the way of furnishings. The floor, marbled stone and wood, blended together in the way the builders made everything, and there was enough space for five people, though it was only Daeven and Peneri left alone, now.

'I will have someone bring you food, and I will send a healer to make your daughter more comfortable,' Orratan said as he left.

Daeven sat on the hard floor beside Peneri, his legs crossed and his back to the wooden wall. She continued to sleep, and he wondered if she would ever wake again. *Was this it, now? Would her eyes stay closed until her final breath?* He wept quietly to himself, trying not to make a sound even though he couldn't hear himself.

He hurriedly wiped his eyes when the curtain to the room moved to reveal a boy of middle-teen years carrying a pair of bowls, their contents steaming in the cold, still air. The boy smiled as he waited for an invitation to enter, raising the bowls a little as if to offer them without the need to speak. Daeven waved the boy in.

Orratan must have told the boy he couldn't hear, as he set the bowls on the floor and immediately used hand-speech. As with all who were branded, Daeven had a mark on his palm, burned there permanently by the orb, but the boy wouldn't have seen it.

'What's wrong with her?' he asked. An innocent question from a young mind.

'She has shanka.'

The boy's expression changed to one of sadness, telling him he knew how serious the illness was. 'I will pray to the Architects for you.'

'Thank you.' Daeven, while grateful for the young man's compassion, felt uneasy receiving it. He broke his gaze away from the boy and looked at the bowls. Two servings of a hot meat stew sat before him. The steam wafted the sweet scent of herbs his way, and though he couldn't bring himself to eat, his mouth watered.

He expected the boy to take his leave, but he didn't. Instead, the boy chose to stay, and sat against the opposite wall, crossing his legs to mirror Daeven's posture. He closed his eyes and spoke gently. His lips didn't move enough for Daeven to understand each word, but he could see he was praying to the Architects. Eraidor, if he wasn't mistaken.

Daeven didn't join in. He'd prayed enough over the past few moons. Instead, he studied the boy. Despite his furs hiding much of his frame, it was evident by his posture he was strong, with good muscle, yet skinny at the same time. The furs didn't hide that. A thin neck on a thin body, though the potential for a tall, strong adult frame was in his future. The red paint in his hair wasn't recent; dark brown roots were showing at the parting, which sat a little off centre. *Those eyebrows would need taming, eventually.* Daeven stifled a smile as a watched on, internally chastising himself for doing so beside his sickly daughter.

'I'm sorry,' the boy said when he'd finished praying and caught Daeven staring. 'Do you wish me to leave?'

Daeven's immediate thought was to say yes, to leave him and Peneri be, but in truth he welcomed the company of this stranger. He told him he could stay a while if he wanted to. 'What's your name?'

'Uehan,' he replied using his mouth, half smiling. 'Are you going to eat your stew?'

Daeven shook his head. He knew what the boy was angling for, so he pushed one of the bowls forward. Uehan hungrily accepted the meal and slurped from the edge of it as if he hadn't eaten in a while himself.

'You should have some,' Uehan said. 'It's very good. My mother made it. She makes the best food in all of Trennale. In all of Dawan... no, all of Rybban! Everyone says so.'

'Is that so?'

Uehan nodded, stew dripping from his chin.

Daeven didn't know what to make of the boy. Clearly he was good-natured, eager to please as any boy should be. Too young to yet have the weight of life's trials bearing down on him. One moon he would be old enough to be Branded, a year or two away, perhaps, unless he had an older sibling, or chose not to. He would make a good healer, Daeven decided. He didn't know why he thought that.

'Please do try it. It's much better when it's hot.'

Far too eager.

Daeven relented. As much as he appreciated the company, Uehan had too much energy about him to tolerate right now. If he ate some of the stew, maybe it would satisfy the boy and he would leave. He needed sleep, and Maera always complained he was more intolerant of others when he was tired *and* hungry.

As he took a mouthful of the stew, he raised his eyebrows. *You know, this young man might be right.* It had been a long time since he'd enjoyed a meal this much. He didn't recognise the meat, though. So tender and full of flavour. He looked at Peneri, and guilt immediately took over again. *How can I enjoy such food while she lay there?* Tear welled again, and he fought to hold them back. *Not in front of the boy.*

He handed the bowl back, barely more than a mouthful taken, then glanced at the curtain and then at Uehan. The boy took the hint and rose to his feet to leave, a bowl in each hand. As he reached for the curtain, a hand from the other side pushed it out of the way. Uehan dropped one of the bowls in surprise, taking a step backwards and kicking the bowl to the wall. The wet contents splattered in all directions, though Uehan took the brunt of it.

A new visitor stepped into the room—a woman so huge she filled the space of two men, and had to stoop against the ceiling. Daeven was a big man by most standards, but this woman made him feel small. Uehan stood, mouth agape at her size. He looked as though he didn't recognise her. She wore dark grey furs the colour of burnt wood, which contrasted a pale face and short, unkempt blonde hair.

Uehan and the stranger exchanged a few words, none that Daeven could make out, then the boy retrieved the wayward bowl and left hurriedly. The woman then knelt at the foot of Peneri's bed, resting her weight on her ankles.

Only then did Daeven notice she didn't have painted hair like everyone else. *Curious.*

'Your daughter is a very beautiful young thing,' the woman said. She used her lips, but he could hear her words in the same way as how Orratan spoke to him. He cocked his head a little. He'd watched her exchange words with Uehan, and she had no companion, and neither of them used hand-speech. *So, not like Orratan?* She wasn't a healer either. Healers couldn't communicate telepathically, and no one in the history of Dawan had more than one ability. One orb, one gift.

'She *is* beautiful, even now. Have you come here to help her? Did Orratan send you?' He spoke with his hands, and she seemed to understand, though she didn't reciprocate.

'In a way, although I am not here to heal her. Shanka is not an illness that can be cured, even by one such as myself.'

'I don't understand. What *can* you do for her?'

The woman brought herself closer to Peneri and stroked the side of her face with the back of her hand in the same manner he would. He wasn't sure if it was the moonlight coming through the window, or his imagination, but he thought he saw light beneath the woman's fingers brightening his daughter's face. Whatever it was—if anything—faded away as quickly as it came.

'Trennale is not the only way. Yes, the Origem resides here within this city, and you all come here from across the land to drink in its power. You all seek the gift of the Architects, though it's not their gift to give. Not truly. That is the secret behind it all, and another secret is there are other ways. The Origem is not complete, no, parts have been lost, stolen. Throughout time they have been secreted away. All over Rybban they are scattered. Some are lost forever, while others are wielded in ways they perhaps should not. It is the secret I offer to you this moon.'

Daeven frowned. He understood most of what she said, but there was a word in there he didn't know. *Origem.* It might have been *origin*, though that didn't make sense to him either. 'Secret?' is all he managed in reply.

'Oh yes, a secret. One that you must not share with anyone else. There is another way to receive the gift you seek for your daughter. I will impart that knowledge to you, but do understand that it is dangerous. It is the only chance you have to save her, and not a good chance. A small one, yes, that is it. A small chance to save her.'

'Why would you offer this if it is dangerous? I don't know you, or if I can trust you.'

'Ah, now I do not give you this knowledge to help your daughter, though it is happenstance that it might. No, there is more at play here than I can share with you. Do you understand?'

'No.'

'I thought not. No matter. If you do as I say, you will be offered that chance. It will still be in the hands of the Architects as to the outcome. I can only *guide* you. For the greater good, you see?'

'I really don't.'

'If you wish your daughter to live, you will need to travel...' She shifted her weight to face away from the bed. With a pale finger, she drew lines in the dust on the floor. When she'd finished, she continued. 'Here.' She pointed to an X she had marked in the centre of the shape.

Daeven scratched his ear, tilting his head to try and make sense of what she was trying to convey. She looked at him, still pointing at her mark.

'This is a map of Dawan. We are here.' She tapped at a triangle. Your village is here.' She pointed to a circle, then at the X again. 'Here you will find your solution. One who can perform the Branding, using one of the lost remnants of the Origem.'

That word again. 'The Branding is only performed here in Trennale. It has only ever been performed here.'

She shook her head. 'You do not know your history as well as you should. The Origem moves. It was once elsewhere. A place in Dawan that no longer exists in the minds of mortals. In fact, that forgotten place was once home to the one you revere alongside the Architects.'

'Dawan, the man?'

'Indeed. Such a long time ago, now. The world was a busy place back then. An important time in history, and the time the world split asunder.'

Peneri groaned and moved uncomfortably in her bed, breaking Daeven's attention away from the woman, whose name he still didn't know.

'She is too ill to travel now. I shouldn't have brought her here in the first place. I can't take her anywhere.'

'And yet you must. I may not be able to cure her ills, but I can make her comfortable enough for this journey. It is imperative for you to go.' She slowly rose to her feet. 'Fear not, for you will not travel alone.' With inhuman speed, the woman reached through the curtain and yanked the young boy, Uehan, back into the room.

'Hey!' he cried, trying to break free.

'Curious that you should be eavesdropping on our conversation, when it is you who are to travel with them.'

'Huh?'

She let go of his furs and indicated the drawing on the floor. 'Do you recognise what this is?'

Uehan paused for a moment before nodding.

'Go with them. Though I must warn you to be careful. There are many dangers you will face along the way. Do not get lost. Do not dally. You all must be there within the span of two moons.'

'And if I refuse?' Daeven asked.

'Your daughter will die, and the world will not be as it must be. I warn you again, do not speak of this to anyone else. For they will prevent you from leaving, and they do not know what it is you must do.'

Daeven and Uehan exchanged looks. 'We don't even know what we must do,' Daeven said.

'Trust in yourselves and you will prevail.' She bowed, smiled, and then squeezed through the doorway.

Daeven would never see her again.

6

'Who was she?' Daeven asked Uehan, as the boy stood there awkwardly.

Uehan blinked, sharing the bemusement. 'I don't know. I've not seen her before.'

Daeven looked at the map on the floor, which had been partially scrubbed away by the heel of the woman's boot. The X remained intact. 'She wants us to go there, although I don't know where that is. I've only travelled between my village and here twice in my life, and have strayed not much farther. Do you recognise it?'

'No.' Uehan wrinkled his nose. 'The elders might have an actual map. I could fetch it for you.'

Daeven's first instinct was to agree and send the boy on the errand, but he hesitated. Dawanii were always taught to help another in any way that they could, but this young man seemed awfully keen to help a perfect stranger in a way that didn't feel right. He wasn't yet old enough to be Branded, and therefore still a child in all sense of the meaning. No,

Architects be damned what the woman said, he wouldn't involve the boy. Then again, he *would* need a proper map. He'd never be able to remember it all.

'Please.'

Uehan nodded and left the room without another breath. Daeven would accept the map and then find a reason to send the boy away, back to his mother and his life here. He would take Peneri by himself. He'd come so far already, and if there was even a little hope left of saving his daughter, he would do so alone. It was his burden alone, and no other.

Peneri tossed and turned in her bed, arching her back and moaning in pain. She wasn't awake, nor was she sleeping. A fevered slumber keeping her away from the worst of her pain, and he could no longer bear to see her suffer.

From where he sat, the white peaks of the mountain glistened in the moonlight, filling all but a sliver of black sky in the window. It stood as the only peak in the otherwise flat and barren plains of Dawan. Every Dawanii child is told of how the mountain came to be—a great fight between all the Architects long before Eraidor created the living.

For when the Architects were all that roamed this world, they squabbled and fought like any family would, except their fights had the power to mend and destroy the lands a thousand times over. Daeven didn't care for those stories now. He prayed the Architects would answer him and save his daughter. He would have them destroy that mountain if it meant she would live. He would destroy the whole world for her.

A shadow moved across the clouds that hung as a ring around the peaks. A small, dark shape—barely more than a speck—weaving in and out of the twin knives that pointed to the stars. That shadow wasn't alone. A second, and a third, more. He counted nine in all, though he could have been wrong. The shadows danced around those peaks like flies around a spoiled meat stew, though he did not figure them to be insects. Birds, perhaps, and then he wondered. *Could they be dragons?*

He'd never seen a dragon, and wasn't sure he'd ever like to now he knew how destructive they could be. He watched, though. He watched the handful of shadows dance in the sky around the mountain of the gods he and everyone revered. These dragons—if that's what they were—had been attacking the city, that first woman had claimed. No story had ever been told of the dragons attacking the world below... not in a thousand years. Not since—

The curtain flung open, and Uehan stepped into the room clutching a roll of paper, half crumpled in his grasp. Daeven beckoned the boy in and reached out a hand to receive the map. He unrolled the parchment and laid it on the floor to study it, comparing the lines to what remained of the crude version the woman had drawn.

There were words written in several places on the drawing in browned ink, though he didn't recognise them. He'd not learned to read—such lessons were not taught to many, and were often left until later in life when one grew close to becoming an elder of their village. 'Can you read these words?'

Uehan shook his head. He pointed to a triangle and then spoke with his hands. 'This is Trennale, I think.' He tapped another spot nearer the top. 'The Sisterhood.' He spoke the names of two other nearby villages, each marked by a small circle, before tilting his head, brow narrowed in thought. He looked at the woman's sketch and the paper, comparing the two, then scratched his head.

Daeven did the same, and at the same time they both pointed at an area on the parchment in agreement that was where the X should be. Daeven wet his finger with his tongue and pressed it to the floor, lifting away some dirt. With that dirt, he marked the parchment, leaving behind a dark mark where they guessed the X should be.

'Almost two moons walk from here, if I had to guess,' said Uehan. He used two fingers to measure the distance between the triangle and the mark of the Sisterhood, which he told Daeven was also two moons away. The new smudge was slightly under the same distance in the opposite direction. 'Two moons,' he said, nodding.

Daeven hung his head. That was still a long walk, even for someone unburdened with the weight of a child on their back. There was no question, though. *Anything it takes.* There was no more time to lose; he had to leave immediately. He turned his back on Uehan and pulled back the furs covering Peneri, ready to lift her from the bed and onto his back. She was soaked through in her own sweat, and her exposed skin was riddled with sores and pustules.

Is this right? Am I making the right choice? He couldn't let her die, yet she was so ill, and the vile disease ravaged her with ever-increasing cruelty. It wasn't even certain she would make it all the way alive. What would happen then? Would he have to bury her in the snow in the middle of nowhere, abandoning her? If she died here in Trennale, she would be afforded a proper funeral under the watch of the Architects. She would have had the same at home, if she'd never left.

In that moment, he knew for certain he'd made the

wrong choice taking her so far from her home, from her mother, and those closest to her. His vision blurred once again from the hot tears that remained ever close since Peneri first fell ill.

Peneri coughed violently as she lay, her head thrown back, arching her spine. Daeven did his best to soothe her. The woman claimed she'd made her well enough to travel, but he couldn't see it in this moment. If anything, she looked far worse, and closer to death than ever.

Uehan rushed to them, taking a place on the opposite side of the bed. He laid a gentle hand on her shoulder as if to steady her from the coughing fit. Daeven tensed, and a rush of heat welled up inside him. He grabbed Uehan's hand and threw it away. 'Get off my daughter!' He shouted, though couldn't hear his own words. The boy recoiled, falling back a step.

'I don't want your help,' Daeven screamed, the muscles in his neck strained with anger. 'Get out! Leave us alone! I will do this alone. This is my burden.'

Uehan sat, both palms pressed to the floor behind him, paralysed in fear.

'I said leave us!'

Quivering, Uehan found the will to move, and scurried out of the room, keeping his back to the wall as he went. As he left, the animal skin curtain fell from its tethering and crumpled to the floor.

Daeven grabbed at the furs on the bed and squeezed his hands into fists, trying to quieten his heart as it furiously pumped hot blood through his veins, his whole body shaking. He shouldn't have shouted at the boy, he knew that. *Too late now.* He was to make this journey alone, and while it wasn't the best way to send Uehan off, the deed was done.

'Time to go,' he said, once his breath had settled. There was no reason to delay, rather if he dallied, he might change his mind. His thoughts rocked with indecision. Deep down he knew he should stay and allow Peneri to live out her final hours as comfortable as possible. In the end, he was unable to overcome his own selfishness.

Peneri wavered into consciousness as he wrapped her up into the makeshift sling that allowed him to carry her on his back. Her eyes were open, and her mouth moved, asking questions he didn't want to answer. She was too weak to fight back, too weak to do anything for herself.

Uehan was long gone when Daeven peered into the hallway, Peneri secured on his back as best as he could manage. There wasn't anyone else around, either. *Would anyone try to challenge me, try to stop me?* He didn't know. Most likely they wouldn't, not unless it was Orratan himself who spotted him. *Could he stop him? Would it matter?*

In the end, he didn't have to find out. No one paid him any attention as he walked through the pathways of the city. Everyone was too concerned with rebuilding everything that had been damaged by the dragons. He looked to the mountaintop, but any sign of the tiny creatures had gone. Soon, he was alone again, out in the snowy wilderness, with the city behind them and an uncertain future ahead.

The moon waned above the tree line. He guessed he'd be able to walk another mile, maybe two before the sky darkened until the moon rose anew many hours later. He had nothing to make fire, nothing to keep them both warm other than the furs they wore. If he wasn't careful, he could die out here alone with Peneri still strapped to his back, and he doubted anyone would ever find them. Fresh snows would come on the wind, and bury them both forever.

He rested against the first tree he reached at the edge of the forest, the thinnest sliver of moonlight remaining. He had no choice but to rest here until the new moon came. Peneri slept. She did nothing else, now. There wasn't anything more he could do other than pray. It felt like that was all he did. Carry his burden and pray to the gods to carry him through.

Maybe he slept, maybe he didn't. There was no way to tell. Amser himself may have stolen time away from him. No sound, no light, no warmth. He could feel the cold, wet ground beneath him, but other than that—and the occasional firebug briefly sparking into a tiny speck of light, as if a star of its own—they may as well be nowhere.

'What have I done?' he cried. He couldn't hear himself, nor could he answer.

With the darkness and silence came the dizziness. There was nothing to ground him, nothing to focus on, and he felt as though the whole world spun around him. Only the wind offered a sense of direction. His stomach yearned for food, yet there was none. That had run out before he'd even reached Trennale, and in his haste to leave again, he'd sought no more. *I am the worst father to have ever lived.* He really believed that, but it was too late to give up now.

After a little more broken sleep—if it was sleep at all—a light caught his eye far off in the distance. It felt too early to be moonrise, and he wasn't convinced the light was coming from the right direction, anyway. The first moonlight *should* come from his left, not right ahead. He considered he might be wrong.

He squinted at the light. It wasn't the right colour for a firebug—they had a pale purple hue to them. This was definitely blue. And it was getting bigger. A tiny pin prick of light grew to a small ball hanging in the air low to the ground. He shifted against the tree before rubbing his face with his hand. The light grew larger… no, not larger… *closer*. Whatever created the light was heading their way. His heart quickened, and he crouched ready with his wall of wind.

What manner of creature is that?

7

The pale blue ball of light changed shape as it approached. It wasn't moving fast, not that Daeven could really tell. Occasionally it would disappear behind a tree as the shape came straight for them. Whatever it was had seen them, he was certain of that. He remained crouched, ready to defend them both is needed. It didn't feel like it was a direwolf, but that didn't mean there weren't a whole host of other possibilities of what it could be. If it was hungry, like he was, it had likely chosen him and Peneri as its next meal.

He doubted he could stave off an attack for long. He was too weak—too tired—for that. No, he'd have to use his defences wisely, putting up a wall for only as long as required, and repeat the move in small bursts until the animal gave up. *If* it gave up.

The shape had four legs, and a tail. It *looked* like a direwolf, though not as big. A cub, maybe. Not an infant, but a younger animal not long away from its mother, looking for its first kill on its own. He tried to swallow, but his mouth was so dry his tongue stuck to the roof of his mouth.

By the time Daeven saw the creature's eyes, the blue light had taken on a life of its own, rippling and pulsing as if the beast was on fire. He *knew* these animals. He'd seen one before, a long time ago when he was younger than Peneri was now. *A cinderfox.*

Twenty years ago he'd been exploring outside the village —against all advice from the elders—with Telmin. They hadn't strayed far—no more than a mile through some of the denser scrubland towards the darker west. It had all been Telmin's idea, but he'd been eager to follow him. On more than one occasion had he got stuck up a tree, and Telmin had to fetch someone from the village to rescue him. He'd do it again anyway. It was while up one of those trees he'd spotted a cinderfox prowling through the vegetation beneath him.

That cinderfox had sat at the bottom of the tree and watched, mouth open, panting. It was as if it was laughing at him as he clung awkwardly to the rough, damp branch he found as his refuge. The cinderfox didn't make a sound, didn't move. It sat and watched with a strange blue flame cresting its entire body. By the time Telmin returned with help to rescue him from the tree, the fox had padded off into the depths of Dawan, never to be seen again.

At the time, Daeven didn't know it was a cinderfox. That name was given to him later when he recounted the tale to the elders. They didn't believe him, since no one had ever seen one before. A creature of myth from times of old. Hundreds of years ago when the lands were one. Daeven knew what he saw, though, even if no one took him at his word.

Daeven had forgotten about that moon, until now.

The cinderfox approached, not cautiously, but not with any hurry either. It looked identical to the one from memory. The ears had the same pattern of black flecks to the tips, as though they had been dipped in pitch. The fire was the same shade of blue, and it even looked at him in the same way—mouth open, tongue out a little. A big, fluffy brush of a tail swung lazily behind it.

Daeven moved his arm in a slow, circular motion to create a shield of air, which barely had the strength to maintain. The animal didn't look like it meant to attack. If anything, it looked grateful to have some company on this dark and desolate night.. It must have sensed the wall, as it sat on its hind legs, tail flicking back and forth a good few feet from the barrier. Only the one casting the sound barrier could see them. To anyone else, even those also able to cast such things, they were invisible. To the creator, their view shimmered as though looking at a reflection in still waters.

Their eyes locked in a tentative gaze as they each took the measure of the other. Two bright bronze eyes stared back at him, brighter than they should have any right to be in this darkness. The blue fire clung tight to its fur, and Daeven felt no heat from it. In fact, he felt nothing at all. Any sense of fear had evaporated along with the loneliness that had accompanied him on his quest. The cinderfox didn't blink, and nor did he.

Dare I lower my defence? He could only hold it for another moment or two before it would fail on its own anyway. Carefully, without sudden movement, he lowered his arm and let the wall disperse into the wind. The cinderfox didn't move.

Daeven spoke a hello to the animal, though he didn't expect it to understand. The cinderfox responded by standing, and he would swear to the Architects it became smaller as it did so. Maybe a handspan less in height, no more, if at all. It kept low, and took a step closer to Daeven, being as cautious as its company. Daeven moved his back to the tree, and placed an arm in defence over Peneri.

The fox then did the last thing he would ever expect. It nuzzled its way into the space between father and daughter, and curled up, tail tucked under its body. The gentle blue flame faded into a strange orange hue. For the first time since leaving Trennale, Daeven found warmth in the guise of an animal most would claim didn't exist. No one in the village would believe this if he told them, and even he struggled to believe it himself.

He carefully placed his hand in the fur, and stroked from behind the ears across its body. The flame didn't burn, nor did the fox complain. In the cold, dark wind, he considered if the cinderfox had saved their lives that night, for all he could do was close his eyes and let the harsh bitterness of nature try to claim them. He closed his eyes and slept, a newfound friend protecting them both.

Daeven rarely remembered his dreams once he woke, but during them, they were as lucid as any memory from the waking world. Since Peneri had taken ill, he'd hardly allowed himself to sleep at all. Not properly, for fear of not being there if she needed him. This night, he dreamed.

In the dreamworld, he heard everything. There was no Branding here, and his hand bore no mark. This was the realm of Soma, the Architect of Dreams. Soma was *everyone* here. Every thought, every person, every animal and tree. All were manifestations of that Architect. To converse with another in the dreamworld was to converse with Soma herself. At least, that is the lesson taught to all as children.

All Daeven's dreams began in the same place—a world full of tall buildings unlike anything anyone had ever seen in the waking world. The wind sang in the air, and the sky was a bright blue without ever a cloud. No moon lit the sky. Instead, a brighter, smaller orb of fire glistened against the smooth surfaces of the world around him. This place had no proper name, and no one Daeven had ever spoken to about it had experienced anything like it, either. The elders theorised it was nothing more than his imagination creating a safe haven for him, but he liked to think this was the true home of the Architects, though he could not prove it.

Beneath his feet was a carpet of green. Thin, tightly packed leaves grew from the dirt, spreading out as far as the eye could see. In this dream, this night, he was alone. Except for the cinderfox that had saved him from the dark.

'Hello again,' Daeven said.

'Hello,' the fox replied. A soft voice, neither male nor female. Daeven knew animals didn't speak, and this one wasn't truly speaking to him now. A construct of his dream to help process the world around him. Part imagination, part Soma. Soma was everything here. Everyone. *Everything.*

'Why are you here? You saved us, me and my daughter, in the waking world. And you are here, too. What manner of creature are you?'

'You needed me, and so I came.'

'But how did you know?'

'I did not. Not in a way you would understand. I am a guide. I am only there when I am needed. You needed me, so I came.'

'What is your name?'

'I have no name. You may name me, if you wish. To everyone I am different.'

'Are you Soma?'

The cinderfox smiled, if animals could smile. 'What do you think?'

'I think I wish my daughter to live. I think I would beg for the Architects to save her. She doesn't deserve to be in such pain.'

The cinderfox looked to the side, and Daeven followed its gaze. There, walking towards them both was Peneri. She looked well, whole, and happy. Her long golden brown hair was unpainted, and she wore a flowing fabric, akin to what the stories told the peoples of ancient times wore, for it wasn't cold here.

'Father,' Peneri said, with a smile as wide as the world. He could only imagine if this was how her voice sounded in the waking world.

'My beloved.' Daeven embraced his daughter, and she nestled her head into his chest. Father, daughter, as close as any bond would ever be. Here in the dreamworld, no illness would touch her. Oh, how he wished he could stay here for all time.

'Can we stay?' Daeven asked of the cinderfox.

'You know the answer to that already. You have to return to the other realm, for you have work to do. You have been set on a path. One you started on your own, yet one that had been determined for you long ago. Trust in all you see, and believe nothing. There is more in the world than you will ever know, and you have a role to play within it. A small role, but an important one nonetheless. Stay on your path. Do what you set out to do, and know that you are right to do so. I came to see that you continue on.'

Daeven considered the cinderfox's words, and frowned as he did so. He felt something in his hand, and saw it was the map given to him by the boy. *How had that got there?* He opened it and saw that it had changed. It was no longer a simple outline drawn in ink, but a perfect image of the world if seen from above. It was almost like looking through a window to another world.

'Observe and remember the way you must go. Do not get lost—wrong turns lead to much danger. Your kin needs you to be strong. The whole world needs you to be stronger.' The cinderfox's mouth didn't move when it spoke. And those were its final words, for it winked, then turned and padded away through the short, neat forest of green earth, taking the blue fire in its fur with it.

He watched the animal fade into the distance between the towering buildings, before kissing Peneri on the forehead, eyes closed. When he opened them again, the cold of the night had returned, and he was once again under the tree. Peneri still slept beside him. The cinderfox, however, had gone.

8

The conversation with the cinderfox in his dream faded from his memory—as all his dreams wont to do—as the gentle glow of a new moon caressed the horizon through the trees. The new light brought with it a sense of renewal, of hope and determination. All the doubts he'd had the moon before were gone. He looked at the map with its crude shapes and lines, though he had a sense of the sketch being something more, once.

There wasn't any sign of the companion animal who had come to visit in the night. The furry stranger who offered warmth and safety on the darkest of nights. He'd have liked to have thanked the fox for its protection, and wondered what it would have said in return, could it have spoken. Animals couldn't talk, though, he knew that. And yet...

Only when he moved to check on Peneri did he notice the dead rabbit lying in the snow where the cinderfox had been. The fur had been stripped roughly from the body, save for the hind legs and head, and steam rose from its exposed flesh. Daeven prodded at it with a finger, and realised it had been cooked somehow. *Had the cinderfox done this?* Had it killed a rabbit, torn away its coat, and then used the heat from its fur to make a warm meal? An impossible notion, yet the evidence was in front of him, plain and simple.

He picked the sorry-looking animal from the ground by a foot and sniffed it. The meat smelled good—no rot or decay. With his free hand, he dug his fingernails into the flesh of its hind leg and pulled the meat from the bone. It came away easily, and gratefully he ate it. Rabbit meat, he found, was usually tough and chewy, but this meat melted in his mouth like the best chickens in his village.

He made to offer some to Peneri, but she was still asleep beside him. He'd not seen her wake since they left Trennale, nor was he convinced she ever would again. Peneri would have adored the cinderfox. She loved all animals, big, small, furry or scaled. It didn't matter to her. She would have given it a name, too.

He ate half of the rabbit before stripping all the meat he could from the remains to save for later. Not for him, but for Peneri should she ever wake. For water, there wasn't anything other than the snow around them. He scooped the freshest and untouched snow he could find and ate some. He allowed a handful to melt in the heat of his palms, and dripped some into Peneri's mouth. She may not be able to eat, but he knew she had to drink to keep hope of her staying alive.

His best guess at studying the map told him their destination was still better part of half the moon away. If he made good progress, with no detours, distractions or other diversions, he could make it there before moonset.

With Peneri strapped once again to his back, he set off through the wastelands of Dawan, alone, tired, but full of determination to make it all the way to the end, even if it killed him in the process. Better for her to live than he, if it came to that.

The moon shone brighter, it seemed, larger than he'd ever known. It still hung low in the sky, barely a sliver of it eaten by time as it climbed higher. It bathed the world in an ethereal glow that cast long shadows everywhere. It was never as bright here as the Old Land on the other side of the Separation, and he'd often wondered why the sky darkened over their land. The elders had their way of explaining it, with tales of abandonment by the Father—the sun that favoured the Old Land, the moon—Mother—willing to keep watch over the lands he didn't want. Daeven wondered if there was a more elegant explanation somehow, yet if there was, it remained elusive.

After a while, a feeling started to gnaw away at him as he trudged ever forward, occasionally checking the map to see if he was still heading in the right direction. Though, if he had to be honest with himself, it was hard to tell. The best he could do was to try to keep a straight line and hope he was correct. The feeling itched away at his mind and whispered to him. *You are not alone out here.* There wasn't anything around for miles. Every now and then a shadow would catch his eye from a distance, and he might convince himself it moved. A small animal, perhaps. He wouldn't allow himself to be distracted. If he stopped and investigated every little thing that moved, he'd be forced to stretch his journey out for another moon. Peneri didn't have time for that.

The feeling refused to go away, reaching the point where he was convinced there was something there with him. The cinderfox, maybe, with its white fur easily disguised against the snow. Even the blue flames may be hidden by the soft blue moonlight. *No!* There, behind that tree to his right, a shape not of an animal. There was someone there, definitely and without question. He pulled the knife he was never without, and for the first time that moon, he deviated from his path.

'I see you.' He shouted, hoping his unheard voice was loud enough.

He stalked the tree he knew concealed the person following them. A small, dark shape, distorted by the light—but certainly human—gave them away, trying their best to keep still and hidden.

'Step out slowly, or by the Architects I will kill you where you stand.'

The shadow moved, just a little, as if whoever it belonged to was trying to decide if it were better to run or surrender. Eventually, with Daeven closing in with each stop, the stalker stepped out.

'You!' Daeven relaxed his arm and returned the knife to his belt.

Uehan carefully used his hands to reply. 'I didn't mean to frighten you. I mean to come with you, to the place the woman talked about. I mean to ask them to Brand me, too.'

'How long have you been following us?'

'Since you left. I kept a distance. I didn't want you to force me back to Trennale, but was too scared to ask you to take me with you, since...' He hung his head.

Uehan was right. If he'd asked to come with them, he'd have said no, and if he'd spotted him earlier—much closer to Trennale—he would have sent him back. Now, he had no other option than to bring the boy with him. The wastelands were too harsh, too dangerous for a boy, even in spite of him making it this far on his own. *Or had he?* Had Uehan been close by the whole time that if he'd got into difficulty he'd have made himself known?

'I don't have enough food for all of us,' Daeven grumbled. He resumed his journey back to the path he'd chosen.

Uehan skipped ahead until he put himself in Daeven's line of sight so he could communicate, walking backwards through the snow as he used handspeech. 'I brought food,' he said, tapping a small but heavy-looking pouch on his back.

Maybe having the boy with us isn't so bad after all. He sniffed a nod and kept walking. There'd be time to stop for food and water later.

The three of them marched and trudged—side by side—with Peneri carried on Daeven's back until the moon reached its apex. Half the moon already gone, and still the landscape hadn't changed from its mix of woodland and emptiness. They walked through dense forest and open skies until Uehan tapped him for attention.

'I think we're heading the wrong way. May I see the map?'

At first, Daeven dismissed his concerns, but the boy grew more insistent, demanding to see the map—to the point he tried to snatch it from his pocket. It was in that moment he felt a flash of anger he struggled to suppress. Not anger at Uehan, more at everything. He was angry at the world, angry at the Architects, and most of all, angry at himself. None of them should be here, out in the world alone, with a dying child on his shoulders.

'Fine, have the map if you must,' he said, relaxing his posture to show he meant no harm towards him. 'This is the right path, I can promise you that.'

Uehan studied the map, glancing around at their

surroundings and drawing imaginary lines on the map with his finger. 'No. We should be here. I think we are here.' He pointed out two spots on the drawing, neither all that far apart in principle, maybe the distance of two fingers-width. In reality, that would likely represent many miles.

'Are you sure?'

'Yes. We need to walk that way.' He pointed to a line of trees. 'There's a village there, maybe they can help us, or at least let us rest safely for a while.'

'I don't want to rest. I don't have *time* to rest,' Daeven protested, although, passing through a settlement wasn't the worst they could do. He nodded, and indicated for Uehan to take the lead.

The strangest thing happened as they grew closer to the smudge on the map—it started to snow. Not just a few flakes whisked into the air and swirled around. Proper snow, almost a full blizzard. except the sky was clear. The moon still shone, and through the falling snow there were still the stars watching over them. It shouldn't be snowing, yet there it was.

Snow was part of their lives, and a snowstorm was nothing new, but there should have been clouds. Uehan didn't seem bothered by it, but Daeven felt as though something was off. Maybe the blizzard was a warning. Maybe it was a sign to keep going, to push on. He had no choice other than the latter, so on they went, leaning into the torrent of large, fluffy snowflakes that descended on them.

The snow clung to them, wet and sticky, covering their furs and turning them into white creatures of the wastelands, indistinguishable from the world around them. Daeven worried for Peneri as he knew the snow blanketed her, too, on his back. They needed shelter, and quickly. His wish was granted, as through the snow he could make out the shape of something that could only be a building. Too wide to be a tree, too tall to be only a rock. A dark shape in the otherwise total white around them.

'Over there,' he said, unsure if Uehan could hear him. It didn't matter, as the boy had seen the same thing and had pointed to it. He too, may have declared his finding vocally. Any moment they would be greeted by strangers, their own kin, who would welcome them from the storm, and offer food and warmth, and a chance to rest briefly before continuing on. The map told them they didn't have much farther to go, but they had no choice other than to stop. Certainly they would have a healer who might offer a little help to Peneri, enough to keep her going for a while longer.

'This isn't right,' Uehan signed, turning in a full circle as he walked without stopping.

Daeven nodded an agreement. Something was off. The dark shape he'd seen turned out to be the corner of a broken stone square. Not shaped or sculpted from its surroundings. *Built.* Many smaller, irregularly-shaped stones stacked on top of one another—or at least, that's how they'd been a long time ago, now covered in vines and moss, disintegrating with age. Abandoned.

They kept going slowly, with caution, and then the snow stopped. At least, it did in the space in front of them. Behind, it continued like a wall, and only now did Daeven consider it was nature's way of telling them to keep away from whatever this place was.

Above, the moon cast a soft light over everything in the quietness of a clear sky. Wherever they now found themselves, it was vast. Dozens upon dozens of crumbling structures stretched out in all directions. Whatever this place had been, it was far larger than Trennale. Now, it was wholly derelict, ruined, devoid of life. Somehow, it reminded him of the dream he had last night, except there was no cinderfox.

There wasn't any real place to rest, no help to receive, and no warmth to find.

'Do you know this place?' Uehan asked.

'Our elders spoke of somewhere like this. A city from the old times when the Old Land was still part of Dawan, or rather, when Dawan was still part of the Old Land. There was a war, and there had been a city at the centre of it all called Elmair. This could be it.'

'What happened here?'

'It was a time when the Architects still walked among us. A time when men still fought over land and property, driven by conquest and death. This, if this is the right place, was where the world was torn apart, where Dawan defied the Architects and tried to claim their power for himself.'

'Then what happened?'

Daeven gestured at the space around him. 'Dawan's actions started a chain of events that ultimately destroyed the city and caused the Separation. It broke the world apart, and one country became two. It gave birth to the Branding, and a whole new way of life. The life we all live by, now. It was the end of everything, and yet the start.' He hesitated for a moment, recalling forgotten stories.' We cannot linger here. It's not safe.'

'How do you mean, not safe?'

Before Daeven could explain the potential danger here, the expression on Uehan's face changed from one of curiosity to fright. His eyes widened and his mouth fell open, his lower lip quivering.

He spun and looked for what had caught Uehan's attention. Between the ruins of two smaller structures crouched a large man, tearing at the carcass of what could have been a direwolf. Whatever it was had had strips of fur pulled away, and blood splattered everywhere, decorating the snow in a pattern of painful death. The man hadn't noticed he was being watched—yet. Too intent on feeding from the flesh that should have been covered against the frigid wind that whipped up around everything.

Daeven crept behind the remnants of a broken wall, careful not to gain the attention of the figure. He signalled to Uehan to do the same. The man *did* look up from his meal, vaguely in their direction, but didn't see anything to concern him.

Through a small hole in the wall, Daeven observed, something he'd done many times when stalking deer in his younger years. The man continued to eat, with blood and entrails dripping from his jaw. A jaw that was crooked and distended, accentuating a crooked nose, and one eye that sat strangely lower than the other. The man had no ears, and barely a tuft of lank, dark hair on a ragged scalp. Curious purple lines threaded his skin, altogether a twisted and broken mess of a man.

A feeling of dread washed over Daeven as he realised the fate of the man, and how much danger they were in. *Torn.* He'd never seen one. He'd hoped he never would, such were the stories told to him and everyone else in Dawan. He knew Uehan would know what this man was, too. A living nightmare, and a cautionary tale of the Architect's power.

Daeven pivoted to bring Uehan into his sight, the boy's frightened expression confirming what he already knew. 'We cannot stay here,' he signed, using small movements. Uehan nodded, then pulled his face into a frown that asked, 'how?'

There was a path that would keep them hidden, out of sight, though only partially. It meant clambering over a mound of rubble that would leave them exposed, even if only for a moment. It could draw the attention of the feeding Torn—if they were unlucky enough for it to look their way at the wrong moment. There was no other choice, though. Daeven held out three fingers, then two, then one. Together, they ran.

9

Daeven allowed Uehan to take the lead. Even without Peneri strapped to his back, he knew the boy would be faster. He really didn't want to look back to see if the half man, half whatever it had become, had spotted them yet. A morbid sense of curiosity took over, though, and as he climbed over the rubble, he glanced back. The Torn wasn't there—only the shredded corpse of the direwolf, abandoned.

'Burn the stones!' he mouthed.

Uehan had already stretched a small lead, sliding down the other side of the rubble pile feet first, using his hands behind him to steady his descent. Daeven followed, but lost his footing on a loose rock, forcing him to stumble. He must have let out an audible cry, as Uehan stopped and turned back.

'Keep going! Get yourself out of here.' He knew the words were awkward, broken, hopefully enough to carry on the wind to Uehan's ears. The boy didn't comply, instead choosing to come to his aid. Daeven gestured him away as he regained his own footing.

Uehan waved a hand from side to side across his chest in a sweeping motion, a pained, worried look in his eyes. Daeven knew exactly what it meant. He twisted, careful not to crush Peneri between him and the rocks as he turned. The Torn man was right there, dark soulless eyes burned into the gaze of his own. Instinctively, Daeven brought up his free arm, creating a burst of air just as the Torn lunged for him. The invisible wall repelled the creature enough to escape the attack. Daeven held out his arm, keeping the Torn at bay as it tried to breach it, frustrated at the unseen barrier. They were practically nose to nose, with only a thin shield of air between them. The barrier did nothing to stop the stench of the Torn man's breath—at least, it might have been his breath. Daeven's stomach lurched in protest.

At the same time, something pulled at his other arm. Uehan, urging him to his feet.

'Go!' Daeven cried. Uehan ignored him. 'I can't hold it for long.'

Uehan let go, darted away and retrieved a strewn tree branch before throwing himself at the Torn, splintering the branch around the Torn's head with such force the wood snapped in the middle. The Torn barely backed away, but it was enough to stop it for long enough, allowing them both to flee.

'You shouldn't have come back,' Daeven said. If Uehan replied, he couldn't tell. Peneri jostled around awkwardly, the bindings that held her working their way loose from all the movement. There was nothing he could do about that right now, except use his hands behind him to support her weight.

There was no looking back this time. They scurried through the derelict and broken buildings, not daring to see if they were being pursued. Daeven had lost his orientation, and prayed that Uehan—still out in front—had a better sense of direction than him.

Uehan darted to his right, disappearing behind a wall, only to emerge a heartbeat later, running in to opposite direction across Daeven's path. He lost sight of the boy behind another wall, only to then see him walking backwards away from something. Only when Daeven caught up with him—barely three steps later—did he see what Uehan could see.

He counted eight more Torn, a mixture of male and female, all in various stages of rot and decay. One, a woman, was missing an arm, and another had lost a whole half of their face, somehow. Some wore furs—or at least what remained of them—while others wore clothing from a fabric of some kind, old, ripped, and held together with little more than dirt. Among them was a child, also ravaged by the condition that turned them from human to broken monster. She couldn't have been any older than Peneri. Daeven shuddered at the thought of his daughter becoming like them.

'I'm sorry,' Uehan said, signing the apology, not taking his eyes off the advancing swarm of Torn.

Daeven wanted to reason with them, although he knew that would be futile. There wasn't anything human left within them to reason with. Some time in their lives, they had come into contact with the raw magic that bound the world—the Architect's power—and it had consumed them, taking away every last drop of what made them alive. These creatures were nothing more than empty husks, unable to live, unable to die. They *could* kill, though. The stories were unclear if they had the capacity to turn their victims into Torn themselves. Children made up tales depicting just that, though whether they were simply created in their imaginations to scare their peers, no one had proven. And Daeven prayed to the Architects they weren't about to find out.

'Can you push them out of the way?' Uehan asked. He'd backtracked until he stood side by side with Daeven. 'If we can get past them to that building over there...' he pointed beyond a group of three Torn growing far too close for comfort once he'd finished signing the words.

'I can try, though I barely have the strength to hold a wall.'

'It only needs to be for a moment. Enough to create a way through.' He picked up a rock and threw it at the closest Torn. It bounced off its forehead, ripping the skin, but did nothing to slow its advance.

Daeven broke into a run, and pulled from every drop of strength he could still find to cast a wall of air, which he pushed at the chosen group of three Torn in the hope it would knock them off their feet. It worked—almost. Two of them fell, but a third whose body was all but naked with melted flesh and open, bloodless wounds, remained standing. The intervention was enough to create the space needed to get by, but not before the last one standing grabbed a hold of the strapping keeping Peneri on his back.

He wrestled to pull himself free, with the help of Uehan, who landed a precise punch on the Torn's nose—what was left of it. Successfully through and free, they reached the target building, found a panel of wood that blocked an archway—a solid version of the curtains found on every home in Dawan. The panel gave way easily, disintegrating from age and decay. They'd thought they'd found a safe haven away from the terrifying creatures bent on consuming them, a place to rest a while and decide how to escape this Architects-foresaken place for good.

Except, what they found was open air. There was no back wall on the other side of the wooden panel. No room, no other walls or roof. Just open, empty, snowy ground—with more Torn milling around aimlessly in the ruined city.

Daeven fell to his knees, exhausted, defeated. He cried, his shoulders shaking violently as he could no longer hold back his fear. He'd failed her. He'd failed Peneri and himself, and he had nothing left inside him to carry on.

'No, you cannot give up now. I won't let you,' Uehan shouted. Daeven could see the words on his lips, the muscles in the boy's neck taught, amplifying the words he had no hope of hearing.

'Take my daughter. You may have a better chance than me. Let me go. I will try to stop them long enough so you can escape.' His breathing laboured as he spoke the words, and did his best to sign them with exhausted hands.

Uehan was having none of it, though. He reached under Daeven's arm and did his best to haul him back to his feet. Daeven tried to shrug him off, defeated and uninterested in going any farther, but Uehan refused to let go.

'*You* will bring her. *You* will save her. You've come so far, and we *will* get out of here alive, I promise you.' Uehan positioned his face right in front of Daeven's line of sight, making sure he saw and understood the words.

The boy truly was a blessing from the Architects. If it weren't for him, he'd be wildly off course, heading into the unknown wilderness where they would probably have died from the elements. Despite them now being trapped in a nest of Torn, he knew Uehan had saved them both, for a little while longer, at least.

A renewed energy found him, and he did his best to smile at the boy through his tears. *How to escape, though?* There's no way he'd find the strength to manipulate the air enough to protect them. Uehan wasn't Branded, so had nothing other than what the Architects had bestowed upon him at birth—youth and a dogged determination he'd rarely seen in someone. It would have to do. It was all they had.

Wrapped in each other's arms, keeping upright and staggering forward, they did their best to outrun the Torn as they all centred in on them both. The twisted, melted beings came from all directions now, as if they were drawn to the strangers in their midst. The moon, half-full, lit the broken city like a beacon heralding their end. There was no way out, nowhere to go. This was the inevitable end of all three of them.

Daeven tripped, snagging his foot on a tangled vine half-buried in the snow, and he went down hard. Uehan wasn't able to bear the weight, and went down with him, the loose snow cascading up and into their faces. He felt Peneri slide up his back, her head now pressing against his neck. He could feel her hot breath on his skin, leaving no doubt she was still alive. *Small mercies.* Although, unless they found a way out, it wouldn't matter.

'I feel something,' Daeven said, scrabbling around at the snow with his hands. Beneath him wasn't solid ground—there was some give to it. He brushed the snow aside furiously, desperately, with both hands. Wood. Frozen, rotting wood that barely held his weight. They were above *something,* a hollow space beneath them. With both fists, he pounded at the wood, forcing it to crack under his weight. Again, and again until it gave out.

He locked eyes with the Torn with the missing arm just

as he fell through the hole he'd created, crashing to whatever waited for them below. He landed stomach first, knocking all the air from his lungs, and he smashed his chin on the ground. Uehan landed awkwardly beside him, still gripping Daeven's arm tight.

The light of the moon filtered through to the newly-found space, illuminating a cloud of dust. Daeven tried to move, but found he couldn't. Every part of him on the front sore from the impact, every part of his back—his neck, his shoulders, his hips—groaned from the whiplash. Chin still to the floor, he turned his head to one side to find Uehan.

'I don't think I'm hurt,' the boy mouthed.

Daeven managed the slightest of nods. 'Help me up.'

It took a moment for them to untangle themselves and fight through the pain, and into an upright position. Both of them had suffered bloody scrapes, and Daeven had no doubt he'd cracked a rib or three. Above, the group of Torn peered through the gaping hole, snarling and sneering at them, but made no attempt to come down after them.

With that reprieve, and with Uehan's help, he released Peneri from her bindings so he could check on her. Aside from a small cut to her cheek, she seemed unharmed, though remained unconscious. *Probably for the best.* No child needed to witness the horrors those monsters represented.

Uehan tapped his shoulder for attention. 'What is this place?'

Daeven shook his head. There wasn't a lot to see. The moonlight didn't stretch far, other than to show they were now in a large rectangular room that wasn't entirely empty. In one corner, he could make out at least two skeletons—likely hundreds of years old—chained to the far wall by the ankles with thin strips of rag mingled in their remains. He shuddered and turned his back.

'Door!' Uehan signed, then skipped into the darkness, appearing to have injured an ankle in the fall.

Daeven lost sight of the boy as he hopped out of the moonlight. It was only since being on this journey he hated not being able to hear. In the safety of his village, it didn't matter. Everyone looked out for everyone else, no matter what. Here, in this gloom, fearful for not only his daughter's life, but his own and now Uehan's too, the silence scared him. Above were creatures that wished to kill them all. He missed Maera, and he missed his bed. And there was no guarantee all this would be worth it in the end. He carefully lowered himself to the floor beside Peneri and stroked her hair. Of course it was all worth it. He'd break the world for her if he had to.

A small stone hit him gently in the leg, startling him. Uehan, still shrouded in the blackness, waved with both hands, beckoning him to follow. He'd found something—hopefully a way out. Once again he lifted Peneri onto his shoulders, not taking the time to strap her this time, all the while keeping the hole above him in view. There weren't as many Torn watching them now, and it worried him where they'd gone.

'I've found a way out. No Torn. Clear.' Uehan said.

Daeven held Peneri to him with one hand, and spoke clumsily with the other. 'Sure?'

'Yes! Come!'

The wooden curtain Uehan had found had been a huge, heavy thing. It hung, broken and partially attached to the frame in which it belonged. On the other side was a corridor that light had long since fled from. There *was* a tiny amount of light coming from somewhere, enough to see a way through, now his eyes had adjusted to the darkness. The sooner they were out into the open air again, the more comfortable he'd feel. Daeven disliked tight, cramped spaces, and given his size, they were more abundant than most people realised.

He had a sense they were heading deeper into the centre of whatever this place used to be, and he hoped that didn't mean more Torn, or other dangers that might be lurking. The smudge on the map that represented this place wasn't too far from his final destination, and he couldn't get there soon enough.

Uehan stopped at another of those wooden curtains, and seemed enthralled at how it swung freely open and closed from whatever attached it to the stonework. It *was* novel, and another time Daeven would have studied it to see how it worked. Despite there being no change in elevation, no steps to climb, he was surprised to find the open world on the other side.

They hurried through the snow, scanning for anything that moved, anything that might be Torn. Nothing, except many more broken buildings that had once been centred around a structure that could have once represented something important, now lost to history. It didn't take long to realise they'd lost all sense of direction. The sky had clouded over, losing what was left of the moon. There was still a soft glow above them, but that offered no help.

Uehan gave up first, pulling himself to a stop, resting his hands on his knees to compose himself. Daeven stopped beside him and shrugged Peneri higher on his back, keeping her tight to him.

'We're lost,' Uehan admitted, after a moment of trying to get a measure of their surroundings.

There was an eerie familiarity to this place that Daeven thought he recognised, though where exactly eluded him. No sane person would ever come here willingly, and it was nothing like Trennale. It was only when he caught sight of a flash of blue light in the distance did he remember something from a dream.

'That way.'

IO

Daeven staggered forward towards the light, his mood lifted at what he saw. Sat on a rock—as if waiting for them—was the cinderfox. Or at least *a* cinderfox. *Could it be the same one?* Impossible to tell, though he was glad to see it.

It waited until they'd got close enough to it before darting off, eyes bright, and tongue hanging out the side of its mouth. The animal only ran to the end of a nearby building before stopping to look back, again waiting. It wanted them to follow.

Uehan had apparently never seen such a creature. Daeven could tell by the excited and curious body language, the boy offering a hand in an attempt to coax the cinderfox to him. It didn't react, though. Each time they grew close enough, it ran away a while, then stopped and waited. This repeated many times until the number of ruins grew fewer, and the rubble replaced by trees.

Not a single Torn found them this time. Daeven might have spotted one or two meandering around in the distance, but if they were there, they were no threat or hinderance to their escape. And escape they did. The party of now four were no longer visitors to that decaying place, now returned to the harsh wastelands that surrounded it, hidden it. This time, the cinderfox didn't abandon them, content to pad alongside them as they journeyed.

'Do you think it has a name? Where did it come from? Are there more of them?' Uehan's questions were relentless as they walked. For a while he did everything he could think of to befriend the animal, each one ignored, not letting him too close. It wasn't wary, as such. More 'I'd like to keep my distance, thank you very much.'

Daeven chose not to answer the questions. Too much talking without hearing his own words frustrated him, and his hands were all that kept Peneri to his back. So, he watched the boy in silence as they searched for his destination.

Uehan illustrated perfectly the optimism and enthusiasm of all that he desperately wanted for Peneri. He'd brushed off the threat from the Torn as if it were a long forgotten memory, not an ordeal escaped from this same moon. The innocence and hope of a young man, willing and ready to take on whatever life might throw at him, unburdened by age and experience. Peneri was close to being robbed of it all. All the potential, all of everything yet to come from a long life not lived. And it broke his heart.

Beside Uehan, the cinderfox—their guardian light in the dark that saved their lives. It, too, full of life and energy, almost pup-like in nature and size—smaller now than it ever had been. Oh how he wished Peneri to see it. She would want to take it home. Whether or not a cinderfox would make a good pet, he had no idea. Possibly not.

'Why are you here?' Daeven asked, a while after Uehan had ran out of questions.

'I told you. I want to be Branded, too.'

'Shouldn't you wait until you are of age? Or are you not permitted?'

'I have a brother, and I don't think it's fair he gets to choose and I don't only because he was born first.'

'You're still too young, though.'

'So is your daughter.'

'That's different. Without the Branding, she'll die. You're not dying. And I don't believe that having an older brother is your true reason, either.' He knew it was none of his concern, but a nagging feeling inside leaned on his curiosity.

'You are very wise. You'd make a good—'

'A good elder, yes, yes.' It was a compliment given too often for his liking. In his opinion, most would make good elders once they'd lived long enough to understand the world around them. He forced a reassuring smile to the boy. Once again he'd been too curt with him.

Uehan stopped walking and straightened his shoulders. 'I had a dream, once. A dream where everything was the same, yet different. A dream where everything was *wrong*. I remember seeing that woman there, in the dream, and when I saw her with you, that's when I knew I had to come with you. I don't know why, but I know I have to be Branded, or everything will go wrong.'

Daeven sniffed at the words and continued walking without reply. He wasn't being dismissive. He knew how powerful dreams could be, and there *was* something about that woman. Whatever his reasons, he found himself glad of the company.

With the horrors of the ruins far behind them, the landmark indicated by the map appeared on the horizon—a lone tree apart from a new woodland. A tree that looked different from all the others. The woods were mostly pine, and this one would be a moon cedar. Where the pines were tall and sharp, the moon cedar spread its branches like a storm cloud, its bark a pale silver. It was a welcome sight in the waning moon, and a relief to Daeven to know they were nearly there. Though, he didn't know what he'd be looking for once inside the woods.

It didn't take long to find out, as the familiar sight of a pair of huts, blown and stretched from their host pine trees presented themselves right ahead. It was definitely a village, albeit small. Hopefully it was the right village. Time would tell.

'There's no one here,' mouthed Uehan, turning back after running ahead. 'It's deserted.'

Daeven's heart sank as he digested the words. *No! This can't be right!* 'Are you certain?' He hurried his pace, desperate to see for himself, hoping against everything the boy was wrong.

He wasn't.

The settlement was too small to be a village, with only seven or eight huts scattered among the trees. They part-circled an empty fire pit that had been long since cold, and the whole affair was set in a sloped valley surrounded by trees, unruly undergrowth, and snow-covered debris. There was truly nothing else here with them.

Daeven fell to his knees, wholly defeated. It was over. There wasn't any hope left now for Peneri. This was her last chance. He pulled the map from his tunic and double-checked the markings. The moon cedar. The smudge mistaken for a village that had almost seen them killed. The woods where they now were, and a mark for where home would be—at least another moon's trek away. Too far for Peneri, and too far for him. He knew Peneri would breathe her last here, and there was nothing more he could do other than to pick one of the deserted huts and make her comfortable.

As he moved to release Peneri from his back, a flash of movement caught his attention. Not only his, but Uehan's and the cinderfox's, too. A bird, most likely, flying amongst the trees, nothing more. Except, the cinderfox grew agitated, running around the clearing as if chasing something unseen.

There it was again, a flash of something weaving through the trees, the cinderfox jumping, trying to catch it, its blue flame burning brighter as it did so. Daeven remained crouched next to Peneri—protective—wary of everything going on around him, ready to invoke a wall of air around them if necessary—however long *that* might last with his exhaustion.

He found the thing flying through the air, the bird or whatever it was, and followed it, determined not to lose sight of it. To not be distracted by the cinderfox's attempts to capture it. He watched as it circled around overhead, flickering in and out of the remnants of the moonlight. It didn't look like a bird—its tail was far too long. And then it swooped down, heading right for them. Daeven followed, unblinking. He jolted when he discovered the shape of a man standing not five paces in front of him. The figure had appeared out of nowhere—*hadn't he?* The bird continued its descent before landing deftly on the stranger's shoulder. Oversized wings flapped, pushing the wind away from beneath it until it settled. The bird turned out to be a silver-blue dragon.

'Greetings and welcome,' said the man, using hand-speech as though he somehow knew Daeven couldn't hear his words if he spoke. Fine lines around his eyes hinted at advancing age, though not yet *old*. He wore a smile along with a robed fur cloak, near perfect black in colour. Half his hair was painted white—an uncommon colour, though not unheard of. Behind him, the cinderfox prowled wary, eyes fixed to the dragon on his shoulder. The dragon though, paid no attention, content and settled where it sat.

Uehan, for his part, was happy to remark they were no longer alone, stating the obvious.

'Where did you come from? There was no one here a moment ago!' Daeven said, bringing himself to his feet.

'We have always been here, does the fact you did not see mean that something is not there?'

Daeven sniffed at the question, then returned his focus to the matter at hand. 'My daughter is sick, dying. We have come to seek your help. *Can* you help her?'

'It may be possible. All travellers are welcome here, and we will do as we can.'

'We?'

As he asked, he noticed more people had appeared out of nowhere—it seemed—and were gathering around them. A mixture of men and women, mostly men, all with the same white streak in their hair, though there were all dressed in the traditional Dawanii way—tight fitting dark furs, with open, uncovered forearms. They approached slowly and with reverence, offering a certain solemnity to the whole affair.

'My name is Artien, and we will of course, assist you. Many travel to this place in search of help and guidance in many forms, often when there is no help or hope elsewhere. What do you seek from us here?'

'I believe if my daughter is presented for the Branding, it will cure her. Is that true?'

'A dangerous endeavour is the Branding, and our elders keep that power for themselves... there. Dangerous, yes. The power of the Origem is something the Architects never meant to be concealed away from everyone.'

There's that word again, the one the woman spoke of.

'I believe it should not be held away from those who seek it. To not understand its true nature, this is the real danger, and you have seen for yourself what happens when it goes wrong. Yes, the Origem can consume those who abuse it, but in the right hands, it can do so much good. Yes, I do believe we can help your daughter. May I?' He pointed to Peneri.

Daeven stepped out of the way, allowing Artien to kneel beside her and examine her. All the while the dragon remained perched on Artien's shoulder. Daeven couldn't help but be curious about the creature. It was the first he'd ever seen.

The dragon craned its long neck backwards over its scaled body, and watched him with accusing eyes. Blue scales looked almost black in the darkening sky, and he wondered if they were made of metal. And then he wondered if there were any other dragons with it. From what he knew of them, there was rarely only one. There was something about this one, though. He reached out a hand to it, and it snapped at him, warning not to get any closer.

'Please leave the dragon alone. His temperament is peaceful most of the time, but is wary of strangers. I'm sure you understand.' Somehow, Daeven heard the words inside his head, in the same way he'd heard Orratan's words back in Trennale.

And as though the cinderfox understood, it nuzzled up against Daeven's legs, pushing him back a step. Uehan returned to join them, having been speaking with two of the others.

'They aren't all part of this village. Most have travelled here, too. I think he lives here alone.' Uehan signed the words discretely, though a sideways glance from Artien signalled he knew what had been said.

'Yes, I do believe we can save her. She will need to regain some strength before she can participate in the ritual. I have provided some help, and you will find she'll wake in a little while. Now, are you hungry? You must be hungry.'

'I'm starving!' Uehan grinned.

'Then you must eat.' He stepped aside and revealed a large tree stump laden with fruits and meat of all manners.

That definitely hadn't been there!

Daeven and Uehan exchanged surprised looks as the others with the white hair approached the feast and helped themselves. Even the cinderfox pushed its way through the crowd, tail flailing wildly, before emerging with a hunk of cooked meat. It padded over to the nearest tree, laid down, and chewed happily on the meal.

Daeven *was* hungry, and the smells coming from the food got the better of him, and with Uehan's encouragement, helped himself to whatever appeared to be the most austere —a nondescript piece of bread. Even that tasted better than anything he'd had for a long time. It didn't feel right to take anything more extravagant. Uehan took as much as he could carry, favouring the more colourful fruits.

Trennale was the only place where the Branding

occurred, as far as anyone would say. Daeven had heard whispers over the years of Brandings outside the city, although he'd never paid much attention until now. There had been no need to. This Artien—whoever he really was—clearly didn't adhere to the traditional way of Dawanii life. And there was something about this place that felt *temporary.*

'How does it work?' Daeven asked when he found himself with a moment alone with Artien, away from the others.

'In much the same way as it does... elsewhere.' He paused as though it made him uncomfortable to say the word *Trennale*. 'Unsanctioned, obviously. The Sisterhood would never permit it, nor the elders. They wish to keep the power of the Architects to themselves. They like to keep control over their people. I have been blessed, though, blessed in a way no one ever has.'

'How do you mean?' Daeven was genuinely interested, not only for the safety of Peneri, but to also satisfy his own curiosity.

'Nine years ago, I was much like you. An upstanding member of my village, one much farther in the darkness than here. I was respected, and appreciated in a way far beyond my years. Would it surprise you to know I didn't take the Branding myself?'

It did, and Daeven immediately and without thought looked at Artien's hands for a Branding mark. Artien seemed to anticipate this and held his palms open for him. 'Then how—'

'How am I communicating with you this way? I received a different kind of gift. I had a communion with the Architects themselves once. It was on the moon of my mother's passing. The moment of her passing, to be precise. I felt a *calling*, somehow. Like I had been touched by someone or something incredibly powerful. Ever since that moon, there has been something different, almost as if the Architects are walking with me, or watching over me.'

'They do watch over us, always.'

'It's more than that. Like I had been chosen to be an emissary for them. Since then, I have chosen to help all those who wouldn't otherwise be helped. Those who couldn't be helped. I went to the Sisterhood, and they called me a fraud, a charlatan, and I was outcast.'

'That doesn't answer how I can hear you, in my head.'

'Soon after my banishment by the Sisterhood, I travelled the whole of Dawan. One moon I discovered a lost city, as you have done this moon. Tell me, do you know what happened there?'

'I've heard stories that—'

'Those stories are wrong. A thousand years ago, Elmair was the heart of the whole world. Until *he* came along and destroyed it. The world broke and unleashed a power so great, it almost destroyed itself. I found a fragment of that power, and it should have consumed me, turned me into one of *them*. Yet it didn't. I was careful not to touch it.' He produced a small stone box from within his robes. 'Can you feel it? Can you feel it call to you as it does to me?'

Daeven shook his head. The box was unassuming, boring even, and it gave him no more feeling than any other box he'd come across.

'Are you sure?' Artien lifted the lid, holding the box forward so Daeven could see inside. Nestled on a piece of dark cloth sat an irregularly-shaped lump of glass. Almost transparent, and with the centre sat a tiny red-purple stone that pulsed gently. It had to be no larger than a seed. Still, he felt nothing from it.

Artien seemed disappointed. 'No matter. This is what will help your daughter. This is what guides me, and allows me to perform miracles. Dangerous, though. Oh yes, very dangerous indeed—in the wrong hands. The Sisterhood would very much like to get hold of this. Oh yes. Lock it away forever where it will be no use to anyone. No, I use it to do good. You'll see.'

Artien's attention snapped elsewhere, and Daeven followed his gaze. It was Peneri—she had woken up, her eyes bleary and expression confused. He rushed to her side and smiled, relieved. So many times on this journey he'd thought he'd never see those beautiful eyes again.

'Where are we?' Peneri mouthed the words uneasily, with a failed attempt to use her hands to do the talking, though she didn't have the energy to lift them. Daeven put his hands on hers, telling her to save her strength.

'I've brought you to see someone who might help you. He'll see you right, and then we can go home. Fear not, Peneri, all will be well, you'll see.'

Peneri furrowed her brow as she looked beyond him to Artien, seeing the dragon on his shoulder. The concern evaporated immediately, replaced with a smile, the way she always smiled when she met a new animal.

'So pretty,' she said. 'What is it?' Of course, she'd never seen a dragon before.

'It's not the only creature here,' Daeven said. He clicked his fingers at the cinderfox to get its attention, and as if it understood, padded over, looked up at Daeven before lying beside Peneri, and resting its head on her chest. Daeven wondered if it really *was* fire within its fur or something else, something that looked like fire, but wasn't.

'She needs more rest,' Artien said, offering a hand to lead him away from his daughter. Daeven reluctantly agreed. *Rest is all she has had.* He gave the cinderfox a meaningful look that said, 'look after her, please.'

'There are others who have come to be Branded. Your daughter will have her turn, and in time to save her life—*if* the Architects will it, of course. Would you care to watch?'

11

Uehan showed a keenness to observe the ritual, though Daeven only showed an interest for the sake of ensuring it was safe enough for Peneri.

'Is it the same as in Trennale? I don't see a monument to the Architects here,' Uehan said. Or at least, that was Daeven's best guess from reading the boy's lips from the angle where he stood.

'Ah, the monument. No, that's not required, merely a decorative display of power designed only to reinforce the power the elders claim to have over all others. Please, follow me.'

Artien walked them both, along with two others who had come for their own reasons, to the unlit fire pit in the centre of the clearing. It was nothing more than a pile of haphazardly stacked wood and brush that had been gathered. An array of grey-brown stones and rocks encircled it, no two sizes the same. As Daeven studied it, he realised what it was. It looked so... *clumsy.*

'You have orbs, too?'

'Yes, in a manner. Fret not, for they are also only a symbol. The ones in... the city hold no more power than, say...' he paused while he picked up a random rock from the ground. 'This one.' He tossed it away gently. 'Of course, there are parts that have had to be improvised, and I can assure you it's safe. For the most part.'

'How do you mean?'

'Nothing is ever completely safe in this world. There are always risks, though a life without risks is no life at all, now is it?'

Daeven drew air in deeply through his nose.

'See for yourself, watch, and be invited to be part of the ceremony.'

Artien clapped his hands twice, which drew the attention of those scattered around the clearing. He spoke to them as they gathered, though Daeven could no longer see the words, Artien's back now turned to him.

The men and women lined up around the fire in a circle, hands crossed in front of them, their heads bowed a little. Artien signalled for Daeven to participate, which he duly did, leaving Peneri behind, but not out of his sight. He took a position within the circle that allowed him to keep both the fire and Peneri in view. Uehan stood two to his right, and the cinderfox alert and calm beside Peneri.

Artien rustled around at the base of the fire, igniting it. The smell came first—sweet and inviting, not acrid and bitter like a normal fire—long before the flames. Blue light flickered into life, not unlike the cinderfox, but not the same, either. Tufts of smoke billowed into the air before being carried away on the breeze.

Daeven was happy to see Artien squeeze himself

between two of the women where he could see what he was saying.

'Friends, thank you for being here on this occasion under the watch and protection of the Architects. Through me they bless each and every one of you. Two will be Branded here, with you as their witness. Both have been turned away by those in... the city. Both are welcomed here under the light of the moon. The Architects wish it, and will gladly accept their sacrifice.'

Artien made a gesture with his hand—a semicircle Daeven recognised as representing the moon—marking the beginning of the ceremony. The first chanting began, and Daeven did his best to join in. It had been a long time since his own Branding, and had forgotten most of the song and how the notes were sung. Though unsure, he didn't attract any strange looks from the others, so believed he was close enough.

The ritual followed the ones he remembered in Trennale almost exactly. The chanting, the prayers, the symbolism. All that differed was the monument, and the array of giant statues of the Architects. Trees had to suffice for those, here in the middle of nowhere.

At the correct time, a man of similar age to Daeven stepped forward, and knelt in front of the fire. Ordinarily, this man would be too old to be Branded. Only at the point of adulthood could one submit themselves to the will of the Architects. Daeven surmised this man had likely declined his invitation at the proper age, and had since changed his mind. Whether that was true or not didn't matter to Daeven, and it certainly didn't weigh on the mind of Artien, either.

Then Artien did something that wasn't familiar. He reached into his robes, retrieved something and threw it into the fire. The gentle flames exploded into a rampant blaze filled with colour that settled to a bright orange. Heat warmed Daeven's face as if he'd been standing so much closer. It forced him to take a step back. No one else reacted with the same surprise.

The man kneeling straightened his back, and amidst the chanting, put his hand into the fire. To Daeven, everything looked normal. The fire burned brighter as the man extended his hand into the flames, as it would have done in Trennale. The chanting around the fire continued. Until it didn't.

At the moment Daeven expected the man to scream in pain, the dragon on Artien's shoulder launched itself into the air and swooped low through the clearing, circled the fire and the man. The dragon crashed through the flames, sending sparks and ash cascading in all directions, like it was attacking something invisible within it.

Everything stopped, except the man was unable to retrieve his arm from the fire. He was stuck. He screamed, but not in the way one would when participating in the ritual. This was the true pain—true agony—of someone trapped and unable to escape. The dragon attacked him, repeatedly diving at him, clawing at his face and body. The man tried his best to fend off the onslaught with his free hand, with little success.

All the witnesses scattered. Some tried to help the man, while others fled. Artien remained where he stood, desperately calling for calm, unable to do anything else, paralysed by his own panic.

'Help me!' Uehan called to Daeven, as he too tried to assist the poor man trapped in the fire.

Daeven tried to get a sense of what was happening amidst the chaos. The dragon, growing more agitated, continued its assault on the fire and the man. Daeven ran to Uehan, and the pair of them tried to pull the man free from the flames. Even with their help the man couldn't move.

'I can't let go of the orb!' he cried. 'It won't let me release it. I can't do it, I'm stuck. Please save me!'

It was no use. If Daeven pulled any harder he felt like he'd rip the poor man's arm clean from his shoulder. He let go and turned to find Artien, who wasn't where he'd last been standing. *Where is he?* He scanned the area, quickly, head jerking left, right. *There!* He ran to him.

Artien was in a state of panic, hands to his head, mouthing indecipherable words to himself. Daeven took him by the shoulders. 'How do we stop it?'

'I- I don't know! My dragon! I must save my dragon!'

'Forget the dragon. How do we put out the fire? How do we save the man? Look at him!'

The dragon darted upward, spinning above the fire, creating a spiral of smoke and flame. It reached higher than the tallest of the nearby trees, hung suspended for a brief instant before tipping itself, nose toward the ground, wings tucked to its side. And then it descended, faster and faster, diving at the centre of the fire.

As it reached the flames, it cried out, mouth open. Even Daeven heard *something*, something unreal and otherworldly, muffled by his deafness, yet reaching out to every living thing in the world. It slammed into the fire, exploding the air around it, sending ash and wood and fire in all directions. The trapped man was thrown clear, Uehan too, who'd still be trying to free him.

It all went still, then. Nothing but the wind blowing the scattered debris of the fire through the air. The dragon was gone, and the fire now nothing more than a gentle smoulder in the centre of the clearing. Beside it, the cinderfox, sitting, howling at the sky as if calling to the moon.

'My dragon,' Artien moaned. 'It's gone.'

Daeven waved dismissively at him before hurrying to the once trapped man, who was now on his back some ten paces from the fire cradling his arm. Angry, bloodied welts covered his skin up to his elbow, and his eyes were wet with pain. A streak of blood ran across his cheek where the dragon had caught him.

'Do we have a healer?' Daeven called, searching the faces of those who had remained, only to be met with solemn shakes of the head. There wasn't one, not within their group. Nearly half of who had started the ceremony had fled with no sign of returning.

'My beautiful dragon. What will I do without him?' Artien knelt by the waning fire and poked around with a tree branch he'd found, desperately searching for it. There was no sign. Whatever happened to the dragon, it'd gone for good.

Daeven did briefly wonder how it could simply disappear like that, but his thoughts returned to Peneri. 'You need to reset the fire. My daughter needs your help.'

Artien shrugged, not looking up. 'There'll be no more Brandings here. I'm sorry, there's nothing I can do for your child now.'

Daeven gulped, unsure if he'd read the old man's words right. He hadn't spoken with his mind, so Daeven hoped he'd misinterpreted him. He pulled on Artien's shoulder until he could see his face clearly. 'Say that again. Tell me I didn't hear that right!'

'I'm sorry, friend. Go back to your village. The Architects have demonstrated their will, and they've deemed this moon unworthy to receive their gifts.'

'You can't! I won't let you! If Peneri isn't Branded, she'll die. Surely you can see that? You *must* help her!'

'Must I? Who says so?'

'I do! You promised you would help her.' Daeven snatched the branch from Artien's hand and tossed it away. 'I demand you help her.'

Artien lowered his head, looking away.

'Uehan, help me,' Daeven said. He began rearranging all the stones that had lined the fire, setting them back to how they'd been fore being displaced by the distraction. Uehan looked confused, then sorry for Daeven, before helping him.

'Is there no way?' Uehan asked.

Daeven watched them both as he worked, hoping the boy might help Artien change his mind.

'The Architects have decided. This was a sign from them that should be heeded.'

'You'd let a girl die?' Uehan asked. 'Do you really believe the Architects would want that? I don't understand what happened here any more than I think you, or anyone else, does. My elders always taught me how precious life is, and my mother tells me so, too. The Architects gave us the Branding, and that has to mean something, doesn't it? If Daeven's daughter is meant to die, if that is their will, then let her find out for herself. Help them.'

'You are wise beyond your years, young man,' Artien said. 'Bring the girl, and we will ask the Architects, and we will discover their answer together.'

Daeven signed his thanks profusely to Uehan, then ran to Peneri. He thanked the Architects for finding the boy, and bringing him along on the journey. *To think I sent him away!* He asked them to reward his bravery and determination. He couldn't imagine how differently this could have been had Uehan not been with him.

Peneri was still conscious, though her eyes were dull and tired. Her skin now speckled with all the signs of that cruel disease that threatened to take her away from him.

'We will make you well again, I promise. Then I will take you home to your mother.'

'Papa? I don't understand.'

'You will be Branded, then everything will be all right. I promise.'

'Branded? I told you I didn't want it! I'm not old enough, and it scares me.'

'If you don't...' Daeven struggled to find kinder words, and came up short. 'You'll die. Do you hear me? You will *die.*'

Peneri didn't react with shock; far from it. 'If the Architects will it, then—'

'*I* don't will it! Peneri, please. It's the only way.'

Before she'd formed an answer, Daeven scooped her up once again from where she lay, and carried her into the clearing where Artien and Uehan were waiting.

'What a pretty wolf,' she said, craning to see the cinderfox she'd apparently forgotten already meeting.

'Do you understand what will happen? Artien addressed Peneri, not Daeven. He took her by the hand and squeezed her wrist gently, as if checking for something.

Peneri shook her head.

'It is important the participant is fully committed, else it can go terribly wrong.' The words came to Daeven through his mind again.

'She knows she will die if she doesn't try. Artien, I am her father. I know what's best for her. Please.'

'By your word, then.' He stepped aside and indicated for Daeven to place Peneri appropriately between the stones.

Daeven had to have her sat on his lap so she could remain upright, such was her lack of strength. He closed his eyes as the flames in front of them grew brighter once more. Behind him, those who had chosen to remain had gathered. He couldn't hear their chants, relying on cues from Artien and Uehan for when the time was right.

With his help, Peneri placed her hand into the fire and screamed.

12

Tears rolled against Daeven's cheeks as he shared in his daughter's pain, as she reached into the fire. He thanked the Architects that he couldn't hear her screams, though he felt every moment of it deep inside him. As he'd done so with his own Branding, the voices came to him in whispers, all the voices of the Architects as they communed with them both. At least, that was what he'd been taught. *Who else could those voices have belonged to?*

With his assistance, Peneri reached for one of the seven orbs hidden within the flames. It wasn't his Branding, so the ritual didn't protect him from the fire. Through gritted teeth, he endured his skin burning all the while she made her decision.

As soon as she made her choice, he withdrew his arm along with hers, and the fire immediately subsided. Peneri offered the orb weakly to Artien—as was proper—for him to reveal the fate the Architects had determined for her.

Silently, Daeven begged the Architects not to have

chosen the Orb of Death, for that would seem a cruel twist, having come so far and endured so much.

'The Orb of the Mind.' Artien held high the stone, revealing the symbol carved into it.

Praise the Architects! A rare gift so few are given! Not only would Peneri live, her health renewing already, she would gain insight to the minds of others. Daeven only knew of two others with this gift. Orratan, in Trennale, and Yona.

It was also a gift for Daeven, one that took him a moment to realise—he would soon hear his daughter's own voice for the first time. She would be able to speak to him, placing the words inside his head. He could gain what everyone else—including Peneri—would lose. And he felt all the more guilty for it. *Is this my reward for saving her life?*

With a little assistance, Peneri pulled herself to her feet. Still weak for now, the Branding had renewed her wholly, and the terrible pustules and welts on her arms and face were already well on their way to distant memory. Her first act was to embrace the cinderfox with a smile on her face, and both hands ruffling through the flaming fur. A child's affection for a handsome beast.

Uehan stepped forward with a smile, which turned to a frown of concern when he noticed the burns on Daeven's forearm. 'That looks painful.' He spoke with his hands.

'A little. I've had worse, and it's worth it.' He smiled as he watched Peneri play with the cinderfox. 'When we return home, I will have a healer take care of it. It's a shame there isn't one here.'

'We must celebrate with a feast!' Artien declared, to the enthusiastic agreement of those who remained. It appeared the loss of his dragon hadn't dampened his mood too much.

'Why are you not being Branded? Have you changed your

mind?' Daeven asked Uehan, scratching his temple with his good hand in between his handspeech.

'The holy man says the moon has passed, and there's not enough light. He has offered me shelter, and I will be Branded by the light of the new moon.' He paused in thought. 'Would you stay? I would like it if you both bore witness.'

Daeven glanced at Peneri again before declining the invitation. 'She may no longer be dying, but I need to get her home. There is just enough moonlight left to get us there. Our village isn't far, all things considered.' He chuckled to himself. 'If I'd known of this place before, I could have saved a lot of time and hardship.'

'Yes, although we would never have met, and I may not have come.'

'True, true. I believe the Architects have a design for us all, for better or for worse, and whether we know of it or not. I am glad to have met you, Uehan. Be well on your journey.'

'I am glad to have known you, too. May the Architects watch over you, always.'

Daeven smiled, nodded, and allowed the boy to go off and search for more food. Though, he'd eaten so much here already.

'Can we keep her?' Peneri asked of the cinderfox. She spoke with her hands still. The change within her would come later, likely by the time they found home.

'Her? How do you know it's a female?'

'I can tell,' she said with a shrug. 'So, can we?'

He thought about it for a moment, but then the decision was taken away from him. The cinderfox licked her hand, barked once, before bounding off up the slope and disappearing into the woods. *Probably for the best. Wild animals make poor pets.*

'Oh,' she said, her expression falling.

'It's time for us to leave. We shouldn't keep your mother waiting.'

Daeven went to Artien one last time, to thank him for his help.

'I am merely a vessel for the will of the Architects, nothing more. They saw the light within your daughter, and chose to keep it burning. Maybe in the future, others will come and see I mean no harm here. That the teachings of those in... Trennale are not the be all and end all. Go in peace, my friend. The Architects do indeed watch over you. They have told me so.'

Daeven smiled and squeezed Artien's hands in his, as was custom, and then left the clearing behind with Peneri beside him. The last of the moonlight showed them the way home. As the glow of the purple insects underfoot outshone the moon, Daeven heard a voice. *Her voice.*

'Papa,' she said. 'Carry me, like you always used to when I was little.'

He smiled and held out his hand. Those words were the most beautiful sound he'd ever heard. A melody carried on the silence of the wind.

THANK YOU

Thank you for reading this novella! I hope you enjoyed it. This story came about as I am writing the sequel to Orchestra of the Gods. I needed to flesh a few things out in that story, and so this novella was born.

Please may I trouble you to leave a review on your preferred platform. I know everywhere asks for reviews these days, but I promise they really do help, especially indie authors such as myself.

If you have not already done so, why not sign up to my newsletter at damien-buckley.com and stay up to date with the latest news and developments as I continue to work on this series. You'll be rewarded with a free ebook copy of *Last Moon of the Timekeeper* as a thank you.

Until next time!

Damien Buckley

1st January, 2026

* 9 7 8 1 9 1 7 7 0 0 1 0 8 *

BV - #0200 - 050126 - C0 - 198/129/6 - PB - 9781917700108 - Matt Lamination